*Letters From A
Kitchen Table*

Letters From A Kitchen Table

John DeFoore Jr

XULON PRESS

Xulon Press
2301 Lucien Way #415
Maitland, FL 32751
407.339.4217
www.xulonpress.com

© 2021 by John N. DeFoore Jr.

All rights reserved solely by the author. The author guarantees all contents are original and do not infringe upon the legal rights of any other person or work. No part of this book may be reproduced in any form without the permission of the author. The views expressed in this book are not necessarily those of the publisher.

Due to the changing nature of the Internet, if there are any web addresses, links, or URLs included in this manuscript, these may have been altered and may no longer be accessible. The views and opinions shared in this book belong solely to the author and do not necessarily reflect those of the publisher. The publisher therefore disclaims responsibility for the views or opinions expressed within the work.

Unless otherwise indicated, Scripture quotations taken from the King James Version (KJV) – *public domain*.

Paperback ISBN-13: 978-1-6628-2786-0
Dust Jacket ISBN-13: 978-1-6628-2787-7
eBook ISBN-13: 978-1-6628-2788-4

Dedicated to John N DeFoore Sr.
"I watched and listened"
My Brother Rick DeFoore
"My Encourager"
Kathryn M DeFoore my wife,
"For believing in me."

Prologue

Fictional

I admire the humble man. He stands the tallest, the strongest in my mind.

Abraham is such a man. He is a searcher, a willing learner, a follower of Christ.

The Bible is made up of such men. As much as we look up to and revere Paul, Peter, John, these were the common men of the days. Not Kings, rulers, Philosophers, but ordinary everyday men.

Abraham is modeled after my father and several other good wise men I have known in my Life.

I enjoyed writing about him.

Table of Contents

Chapter 1 1
Chapter 2 21
Chapter 3 41
Chapter 4 59
Chapter 5 79
Chapter 6 97
Chapter 7 115
Chapter 8 133
Chapter 9 149
Chapter 10 165
Chapter 11 183
Chapter 12 197
Chapter 13 211
Chapter 14 223
Chapter 15 237
Chapter 16 253
Chapter 17 269
Chapter 18 285
Chapter 19 301
Chapter 20 317
Chapter 21 333

Chapter 1

Rustling, whispering
Sliding on the roof
Busy dried memories
Rush down the rusted metal and dance ballet-ed to the ground.

The Oak, the tall barn neighbor,
Shakes herself to a cool wind's call,
And showers over tin and faded wood
Autumn's gold and red rattling breeze riders.

He loved this place,
That's why the chair and trunk.
The only two items in the barn loft
Close to the hay loft door.

One to rest his weary bones,
And one to house the questions,
And maybe the answers
To Abrahams time on earth.

The old canvas covered trunk
Filled with Abraham's treasures,

The Bible, Beyond Good and Evil,
Summa Theologica, Christian Discourses,
several more
Hours and years of reading and study.

The old "Westport" Chair he copied from
a magazine
Was worn and faded
But it still welcomed his old bones.

Abraham 78 years, lived, farmed
Married, widowed
Watching the town of Rayner close its doors
And move away.

This loft once stored hay
But now unused, except for Abraham
Rain or shine until it got too cold
His thinking place.

Peace, completeness, safety,
Sometime Ruthie snorted and lowed below,
The feathered girls argued or bragged of an
egg laying,
And of course the pigeons,
Fluttering in and out of the eaves.

Often visits from Thomas
In search of a quick head scratch,
And the off chance of a
Mouse lunch.

Chapter 1

Thomas's full name was
"Thomas Felinas"
In honor of the Italian Theologian
From the 13th century

The tap of loose tin in the northeast corner,
The hay bale pulley swinging in the wind,
Some might say it was noisy,
Not Abraham.

So, not quiet,
But accepted.
He needed the sound,
Needed it to be there, predictable.

For here Abraham contemplated,
Read, pondered, ruminated.
The Bible, writings of Nietzsche, Jean Paul Sartre, Thomas Aquinas
He was the first to admit what was said was often above him.

Abraham's father had been a preacher for three Baptist Churches
Making his rounds all day Sunday's, preaching.
During the week he was the school teacher,
He was a very learned man.

He had a degree from The Fort Worth Bible college,
But being a somewhat timid man,
Kept most of his knowledge to himself,

Unless you were his only son.

His father challenged Abraham almost from birth
Always asking why,
And supplying books to find the answers

Abraham read and read and read
So deep so much to ponder and question.
Abraham was drawn to farming,
But he didn't leave his books.

They made him think,
Old ideas new approaches.
Depths unexpected,
Filled with what if's and maybe's.

Thoughts for the long rows,
Acres of furrowed fields.
Fertilized by musings of Kierkegaard,
Colored by remembered father's sermons.

Often he turned to a simple read
"God, A Deeper Meaning"
By Heed J Foroon Jr
Not the deepest work
but it made him think

Turns out Mr Foroon was the only living author
In his collection.
So Abraham sharpened his pencil with his
old Barlow,

Chapter 1

Licked the pencil point, and started a letter.

Dear Mr Foroon

I am hoping you could answer a question
Regarding your book "God, A Deeper Meaning".
For instance your statement on page 178 saying
"Hell may be far worse than fire and brimstone, it may be
beyond God".

Of the horrors of hell I have no doubt,
But I was wondering about your thoughts
Regarding "beyond God".

I have found your book very interesting
Giving me a lot to think about.

Yours Truly
Abraham Graham
General Delivery
Rayner Texas

Mailed and almost forgotten,
Abraham still searched catalogs for
Books to fill his hours,
Learning more of God.

Weeks passed and Abraham discovered
A new book "The Screwtape Letters"
By C.S. Lewis
He found it fascinating and educational.

He was starting on his third read when it arrived.

First Monday of October
A visit to Aspermont
Meant Groceries and mail,
There was a letter, from HJ Foroon Jr.

Addressed to Mr Abraham Graham
General Delivery
Rayner, Texas.

He carried it home folded carefully in his bib overall's pocket
A slight yellow appearing through a small hole in his bib.
It was protected and greatly anticipated
as he rushed his homeward steps.

Carefully positioned in his barn haven,
"Westport" perched, he loosened the flap
Of his old bib overalls
and with some ceremony unfolded the pages.

Dear Sir

Thank you for your kind letter.
As is often the case with the written
Word meanings can be lost or misconstrued.
It is a treat to be questioned about my book.
In this instance I was trying to explain
My personal thought process when reading of hell.

Chapter 1

After great thought, self-reflection and Bible study,
I have decided that Man might endure fire and brimstone,
if, and only if, he were able to pray, to scream out
to his Lord,
"My God, my God!" in his pain and anguish.

However, after much study and discourse among
Christian brothers
I do not believe God hears the souls in Hell,
Those remorseful creatures caught in pain and torment.
Therefore what frightens me in regard to Hell
Is being beyond the Love of God.

There can be no greater Hell for man,
than for the Great God Almighty to turn His back
upon man, to stop his ears
to these poor soul's cries of anguish and regret.

The introspective ramblings of an old man, perhaps but
I hope this explains my thoughts and you find it helpful.

Again, thank so much for reading my book
and I hope I have answered your question.

HJ Foroon Jr

Abraham sat back in his chair
Folded the letter and placed it between the pages
and back cover
of "God, A Deeper Meaning".

He closed his eyes and thought
For quite a while
He himself had indeed endured some massive pain
Times of heart-breaking grief
But always found solace and release in prayer.

It makes sense
To be hell
There could be no prayer
No relief

Dusk oranged the sky,
The barn swallows went about their nightly hunt
before turning in,
And Abraham climbed down
The worn old ladder.

He headed for the kitchen for he knew
There was some left over peas and corn bread,
And at 8'oclock an "X" Border station
Broadcast evangelists Aimee McPherson.

Though he didn't often agree with her,
She did often offer food for thought.
She was preaching tonight on the
eighth commandment.

Being early for the broadcast
Abraham sat at the kitchen table
And decided to write HJ Foroon again.
Not sure if his second letter would be read

Chapter 1

he still wanted to write down his thoughts.

Dear sir

Thank you so much for your letter.
I can find no fault in your logic as regards to
The Lord stopping His ears.

My simple thoughts are:

Beyond God's hearing,
Unable to call out,
Beyond the love of God,
Is that possible?

Only if the great "I am" Himself
Stopped His Own ears,
Only by His self-willed deafness,
Could he "not hear".

If we His children have the deep "God given"
Sympathy and empathy we have,
How much greater His must be!
So, Hell must also be unbearably painful to God.

For are we not all His children?
It must be extreme torture to hear even the non-believers

As they cry out, beg, scream, plead for another chance.
I would say that it is still within in my fundamen-
talist beliefs

to accept your premise
And I appreciate your thought provoking words.

It is a pleasure to hear and understand
some of your reasonings regarding this book.

Yours Abraham Graham
General Delivery
Rayner Texas

He could get Horace to mail his letter,
He made trips to Aspermont once or twice a week

Five minutes to 8:00 and it would take most
of that time
to tune in the station.
He sat in Betsy's rocker and reached over
turning the tuning knob back and forth
Searching for a clear signal or as little static
as possible.

He turned on the lamp,
Leaned back in her rocker,
Slid off his brogans,
And crossed his socked ankles.

After advertisements for Houghton
Printing Company
And WM Smith Patent Water closets,
The choir started up with "Bringing In The Sheaves"
And Sister Aimee was introduced.

Chapter 1

Abraham dropped off to sleep

Early Monday morning called.
Abraham's old watch said 4:58
Getting up late was not much of a
problem now days
He wasn't doing any farming.

Just gardening and caring for their small orchard
He and Betsy had always canned together so
he knew how.
Picking the garden would come soon,

Then the orchard,
Gotta have food for winter.
Two of Greta's 1 year olds
Were curing, so there'd be plenty of pork
chops and hams.
It was the first Monday of November

The following Monday,
As a reward for his trip,
The Aspermont Post Office presented Abraham
with a new letter from HJ Foroon.

Too excited to wait,
He sat on the bench in front of
Of the Aspermont Mercantile
And read.

My Dear Mr Graham

Exactly! my thoughts exactly!
Well put, better than I could have said.
We live our lives on the periphery of God's love,
His children by faith our tenuous hold at best.

His–as constant, ours frail.
Attacked, tried, bombarded
By worldly trials
Yet often we still find joy, Love and peace.

For the periphery of God's love,
Is still strong, warming, protective.
Imagine if you will
Being totally in God's presence,
Surely it will be breath-taking!

To call out from hell,
Only to be showered by your own unheard cries,
hurled back as brimstone,
Pelted by brittle rejected pleas.

Surely that would be the true Hell.

Thank you for your thought-provoking missives.

Yours HJ

Lighter steps and thoughts tumbling,
shortened the distance from Aspermont to Rayner.

Chapter 1

He had a strong need for hay loft time.

The following day was chilly
But the chores were done,
and the loft called
So strongly.

Abe got his winter coat, an old quilt,
and headed for the barn.
Climbing the ladder with the quilt was tricky,
He kept stepping on the quilt when going up
rung by rung,

Finally getting there he made his way to his chair.
The wind was pretty strong
And he began thinking that it was a mistake.

Wrapping the quilt 'round his boney shoulders,
He re-read the remains of his last letter.
Then, putting pencil to paper,
Abraham wrote.

A raftered pigeon's view,
Was an old white-haired head, wisping in the cool
November wind.
Quilt shoulders,
He sat hunched over in an old chair.

Paper fluttering under pen,
Abraham was not here at the moment,
More inside his head,

He spoke to a kindred spirit.

A brother of like thought
A suggester,
A mentor,
A thought provoker.

My Dear HJ

*After listening to a Radio evangelist sermon on the eighth
    commandment
A question has been forming.
I have been wondering,*

*Pondering if you will.
To place stealing as equal with murder,
As an equal With Thou Shalt have no other God before me,
A warning against the dilution of the Great I Am,*

*What is the sin?
The importance seemingly trivial
In such august company,
Compared to the others.*

*Six ears of corn from the corncrib of a wealthy man
Would never be missed
No loss recognized,
No harm done.*

*Yet equal in the eyes of the Lord,
With sleeping with another man's wife?*

Chapter 1

Where the harm, where the answer?

Is it the ignoring of God?
The placing of man above God?
Saying "I doubt your ability oh Lord to provide for me,
I will therefore take it upon myself to supply my
own needs,

I have no need of Your help"

Maybe that is the sin
That elevates stealing
To the number eight
In commandments.

What think you?

I hope all is well with
You

Sincerely
Abraham

The letter written and enveloped
Abraham carefully added the address
118 August Ave, Fort Worth Texas.
He then pulled the quilt higher around his shoulders,
For the cold grew.

Today was one of "Those" days

Reflection, wistfulness.
He closed his eyes,
Elizabeth Vivian Camden was her name
The light of the playground.

Abraham read and studied obsessively in school
because Elizabeth loved smart boys.
The brightest in Sunday School,
Again for the blond "Ray of Sunshine"
In the blue flowered dress.

He was not sure when his thirst for knowledge
Slipped from Elizabeth to Abraham driven.
However books, because of his father
And Elizabeth, became his love after farming.

Abraham dropped the "Abe" nickname,
Because Elizabeth said his full name was so musical.
Elizabeth became Betsy because
Elizabeth was stern and Betsy sounded happy.

Marriage and farming a foregone conclusion in
Rayner Texas
But their childless marriage
Cast shadows,
And weighed heavy on the young couple.

Abraham remembers the "day"
He decided it was time.
Sitting at their kitchen table
He brought up what neither one them

Chapter 1

Wanted to mentioned.

He had prepared what he was to say
And started.
"It appears after three years with no children we
may not be raising a family.
Ours is not to question our lot,
But to learn what the Lord might want of us.

We could finish our years in sorrow and regret,
Downcast, bemoan our lives of loneliness,
Or we could turn our love towards the Lord and
each other
And try to be shining examples of God's love for
others to see"

He remembered Betsy's face
Her beautiful smile through her tears,
He remembered her words as she took his hand
"God's wisdom from your lips Abraham Graham"
and thus they had lived.

Twilight had crept up on him
No lunch and long shadows caught his attention.
Leaving the quilt tucked into his trunk of books,
Abraham made his way down and towards his
back door.

A long week of canning,
A must for winter's supplies
The last of the garden gathered,

Piled high upon tables and in baskets
behind the door,
More than he could ever eat, still he canned.

The last case of jars from the root cellar,
Abraham could not remember when they had all been used.
He was exhausted after canning 9 days
Morning to night, he didn't know how Betsy
had done it!

Several nights he'd fallen asleep in Betsy's rocker
Awakening to the sounds of static
And the fading in and out of the border
radio stations.

But it was done
The shelves completely filled
As well as a considerable area of floor
in the corner of the root cellar.

Take that winter!
Salted bacon, hams
The Graham farm was ready
Do your best

December's letter was more personal
Than HJ's last two
Explaining an illness and a struggle
With the infirmities of old age
As a tardiness of his reply.

Chapter 1

Abraham would have to explain in a future letter
Only getting mail once a month
He would not notice a tardiness unless it extended
over a month

My friend Abraham

For I feel we are friends in Christ,
I must apologize for the lateness in my reply.
Age related health problems
Have impeded my prompt reply.

An amazing hypothesis!
Well done my friend
an in-depth understanding of our Lord's message.
It turns a simple selfish gesture into its basic nature.
A doubting of God's willingness or even His ability to care
for our needs.

Perhaps viewing the New Testament from this
point of view
Can shed a new light on the Lord's word.

I believe that envy can be the first step towards theft,
A desire for what you don't have can negate the joys of
what you do have.
Envy becomes simple,
because if what you are envying was good for you
at that time, the Lord would indeed supply it.

Often, I have referred to a Poem

From the late 1800's
Written by Edward Arlington Robinson
"Richard Cory"
It deals very succinctly with envy.

I hope your health is good
Strange how the mind ages so much slower than the body.

Please write soon
Your ideas brighten and enrich my days,
And give fuel for my thoughts.

Your friend HJ Foroon

Chapter 2

Abraham's 1927 Ford truck
Was readied for the trip.
Oil, petrol, water, blankets, tires and patches,
The truck had doors.
Abraham made them, painted them black.

The doors rattled and banged,
But with side curtains
They reduced the winter winds
That so deeply chilled his almost 78 year old bones.

He needed two eye covers for the cook stove.
One already cracked, the second one broke
during canning.
A new oven door, way past time,
Chicken feed, and some medicine for Ruthie,
She was looking down.

Too much to carry walking
And the weather was too chilly.
Better to get it over with
Overcast sky could mean rain.

There were times when he walked
But weather and now days age,
Drew him towards driving.
It appears the calendar dictated his transportation.

The trip would take almost an hour each way
Not a far distance but the wagon ruts didn't fit his truck,
So you couldn't get up much speed.
When it was drier you almost did better driving beside the road.

Abraham left just after dawn,
The truck lights were not very bright
And after about an hour or so
He pulled into Aspermont and headed for the Mercantile.

Mr Rayford had sent word
His stove parts were in.
He bought a few other things
And for some reason or other
A treat for himself
10 cents worth of hard candy.

Then on a whim he went to the Cafe for an early Lunch.
A steak and eggs, 28 cents well spent.
It was rare that Abraham got beef
Unless he could trade for some.
Which hadn't happened lately.

Chapter 2

Starting his homeward journey under a grey sky
with a slight mist
The roads were even more slippery
And the mud began deepening.
A mile from home
He spotted a strange dark lump,
Just off the road.

It was new, it had not been there
When he passed by earlier,
So his curiosity got the better of him.
Maybe a neighbor had lost part of a load.

Stopping nearby
It appeared to be somebody
Under an old blanket.
He "hello-ed" only, to see a small face
Peering out.

He walked to the blanket,
Pulled it back to find two children.
They appeared to be two girls,
An older and younger,
Shabbily dressed.

They were curled together
Trying to find warmth under the wet blanket.
After asking about parents and home
With no answer,
Abraham picked up the younger of the two
And placed her in the truck seat.

The older followed, getting in only when told to.
He got the dry blanket he had brought
for emergency
And wrapped them together in the front seat.

He started once more for the house
With two little mysteries on his truck seat.
Arriving in 25 minutes or so
He gave them separate dry quilts,
But they preferred to squeeze together under one.

He replaced the two stove covers,
And the oven door,
Which he had to do when the stove was cold,
Then lit the stove and boiled water.

The kitchen soon warmed up
And the children's shivering lessened.
He made two cups of half coffee half milk,
Added two large spoons of sugar,
And handed one to each child.

They blew and sipped noisily.
Abraham had a suspicion they hadn't eaten lately
so he fried up some eggs and bacon.
They each ate as fast as it would cool and they
could swallow.

Only moments after the food was finished
eyelids drooped
Yawns and nodding began.

Chapter 2

It was not the time for questions or bathing,
So he led them to the guest bedroom, that's what
Betsy called it,

Rarely used but still Betsy's pride.
They climbed in bed and Abraham
Covered them up.
Returning to the kitchen table
Abraham realized
He was lost!

Bamboozled, stymied, flummoxed.
Totally unfamiliar with children,
No idea what to do with two little girls.
He would have to talk to the marshal,
Back in Aspermont.

Find their folks,
First thing in the morning.

Then on the kitchen table
He laid a piece of paper and a pencil,

My Friend HJ

I am a selfish man
I live my life as if it was all about me.
Then I try to pray,
God must be aghast at my blindness.

*Can it be
Is this a pattern?
Do all sins
Lead from Self?*

*I find my Self always standing
Between me and God
I can repeat the words
"Die to self"*

*But most often
These words are bitter on my tongue,
For upon opening my mouth
I once again am revealed in self.*

*I believe self to be the catalyst,
Why we envy,
Why we Lust,
Started by excluding God.*

*If I open my mouth
For any reason other
Than to speak Christ-like,
I once again am in self.*

On another note,

*I have come upon a problem.
This day which caused me to ask,
Why me Lord
Why disturb my life, my comfort?*

CHAPTER 2

Self once again revealed.

Never did I say Lord show me,
Lord grow me,
Never praised God's wisdom,
Or looked forward to the lessons and growth
to be accrued by this challenge

Self is indeed blinding me to God's gifts,
To give myself over to praise,
To thank him for this challenge
To love and accept His plan.

Here I am once more, standing in my own way.

The bigger the challenge
the greater chance to learn,
To praise God for this chance to grow,

And I do have a large chance to grow.
Please forgive my rant,
My new traces chafe,
And I balk at the load.

Drive me Lord, I will go.

I do hope you are continuing to mend,
And look forward to hearing from you.

Yours in friendship
Abraham

Turning out the light
Abraham went to bed,
To the familiar creak of the springs.
He was so tired this night

And he missed Betsy so.
Sleep came quickly.

Othello crowed loudly,
Bragging, strutting,
Knowing only he could raise the sun,
He called the light into being.

Abraham started the kitchen fire,
Went to gather eggs,
And secure some of Ruthie's milk.
He had bought bread so there would be toast.

He cooked and waited,
And waited.
He went to the bedroom door and knocked,
No answer.

Slowly he opened the door
To find the bed empty,
And the two little girls
On the floor in the corner
Under their dirty old blanket.

He asked the elder if they would come eat breakfast
They just sat.

Perhaps a little frustrated Abraham
Used the word "Now" firmly,

At which they immediately scurried into
the kitchen
and stood against the wall.
Abraham seated them both
In front of their breakfast
And said "eat".

Crumbs flew, eggs sucked down,
Bacon stuffed into overfilled mouths,
Milk inhaled two glasses each,
And slowly they stilled.

They looked at Abraham expectantly, fearfully,
And waited.
He asked the elder, what can I call you?
She responded in a wispy, airy voice, my
name Hannah.

Abraham said "hello Hannah my name is Abraham"
Hannah quickly responded "Like from the Bible".
He smiled and said "why yes and what is you little
sisters name?".

"He's my little brother Pa just never cut his hair,
His name is Issac,
like from the Bible."

"Where are your folks they must be worried"
Abraham said,
Hannah quickly answered "Maw is dead,
She went to heaven when Issac was born",

"Pa's gone to California .
We figure it's the next town over,
He said we should find somebody
To take care of us, he let us out of his truck
on the road
Then God sent you".

Issac was scared of you but I knew you were kind"
Otherwise God wouldn't of sent ya would he"
And Abraham just stood there.

After breakfast Abraham made
A return trip to Aspermont,
With the children in the truck.
Abraham talked with the Aspermont Marshal.
He soon discovered the nearest place to house
orphans was Fort Worth.

Most of the time orphans went to other
family members
Or sometimes a Church member would
take them in.
The old marshal looked at the two children in
the truck,

He spat a tobacco chaw out,

Chapter 2

Then dug around in his check with his finger,
Flicking the residue on the ground and
truck fender.

"If'n you don't want'um, I reckon the best idee
would be turn'um loose
let 'um fen' fur themsel's, that old'un there peers
like she's old e'nuff.
Just don't turn'um loose in my town!
Then go home an forget about it"

Abraham stopped by the general store
Bought two dresses, a pair of girls shoes, a
nightdress
Two pair of pants with room to grow.
Shirts, boy's shoes and boy's night shirt
Some ribbon and some pomade.

It was a quiet ride home
Betsy would be crying with joy, if she were alive.
Abraham felt 78 years old is too old to raise kids,
Though this was a chance to have a
daughter and son.
He did worry about his loft time though.

Arriving back at the farm
Abraham cooked supper,
And then pulled the old galvanized bathtub into
the kitchen.
Hannah took over heating water.

Issac and Abraham went into the parlor to give
Hannah privacy,
Then it was Issac's turn.
Hannah rewarmed the water,

And oversaw Issac's scrubbing,
Though she let him do it himself.
When he was finished
Abraham was surprised to see them drag the tub
out together and empty it.

They then brought it back in and Hannah began
filling it again.
Abraham asked "Hannah, what are you doing?"
"I was fixin your bath sir,
Cleanliness is next to Godliness" my mother
always said.

Abraham was surprised, touched.
It had been quite a while since someone had
"done" for him.
Betsy had
But not since.

Abraham put them to bed
And took his bath
It was different,
Someone had prepared it for him.

He sat at the table after dressing for bed
And wrote again

Chapter 2

My Dear HJ

I know you haven't received my letter and here I am writing again,
I just have more to say.

I have been undone!
Our God has seen fit to unmake me,
To change my life,
My pattern,
And ask so much more from me!

On the way home from a town nearby
I came across two unattended children,
A girl 11 or 12 years of age,
And a boy about half her age.

Their father had left them beside the road
And gone off to California.
I have been unable to find a place for them,
So it appears as if at 78 years of age,
I may be raising two children.

I have no doubt,
Not for a moment,
That this is the Lord's will,
That this is His plan.

So my task is plain,
Grow in the Lord.
Recognize the blessing

The Lord has given me.

I fight against this!
It is a battle,
I long for my aloneness,
Yet am deeply touched by a small kindness
from the two children.

Has all I've read, studied
Been the minor lessons,
Preparing me for this greater?
To follow blindly
Only in faith?

To step out on the untrodden path,
Leave behind my comfort, predictability, familiarness,
To say Lord I will follow where you lead
no matter the path.

Your friend on an unchartered Journey

Abraham

Next Monday Abraham would mail this letter
And hopefully receive a letter from HJ.
Now to bed for Othello's crow will not come late
And there's a talk to be had with the children.

Abraham woke to Othello's braggadocio
In calling up the sun.
So naive and full of himself

Chapter 2

(Perhaps food for Abraham's own introspection)

Started the fire, coffee then bacon
By the time he was starting the eggs
Hannah appeared in the doorway
Sleepy eyed with her new pink flowered
nightdress on.

Abraham asked her to wake Issac.
They blessed the meal
And ate in silence.
Abraham had not had conversations
For quite a few years.

Hannah helped with the dishes
Then Abraham escorted them into the parlor
Had them sit.
They looked nice in their new clothes,
Though Issac's hair was still unshorn.

Abraham began
"My name is Abraham,
I live here alone,
My wife Betsy passed away 10 years ago.

I talked to the marshal
Yesterday about finding a home for you two
But as far as I can tell,
There is nowhere but here.

I can take y'all to some nearby towns and churches

And look for a family,
Or you can live with an old man.
You'll have to help me though.

I will welcome you here,
I believe it to be the Lord's plan
But I want you to have a say
And I want to know what you think.
 So Hannah
What have you to say?"

"Hannah paused then said
"Issac and I talked after you fixed us
 That first breakfast.
 Issac said you had a kind smile.
 And you've been nicer then anybody ever was to us.

We would like to stay with you.
We're good at chores,
We'll be quiet, and stay outta your way
if you let us stay"

It was agreed
They all smiled
Went back in the Kitchen
Hannah cleared the table,
Abraham washed and Issac dried
Then the three went to do the chores.

In the evening
Abraham found Betsy's scissors,

Chapter 2

The one's he used on his own hair
And with Hannah overseeing ,
They cut Issac's hair.

Monday morning arrived and they bundled up,
piled into the truck
And headed for Aspermont.
Abraham had a large list,
Coats, hats, other clothing.
The children loaded boxes in to the back
of the truck
And after paying the bill
Abraham handed each child a dime,
Saying "See if you can spend this on yourselves".

They just stood there,
A dime in each child's hand.
Abraham repeated saying
"Go back in the store while I wait out here
Buy whatever you want".

Abraham finally opened the store door
And gently pushed each child in and
closed the door.
He then went next door to the post office
to retrieve his mail and mail his latest letter.

They were standing by the truck when he returned
He said, "let's load up"
Then he said "are you ready to go home?"
They nodded

And they were off.

Each had a small bag of hard candy
Which they shared back and forth
And kept them occupied
For most of the trip home.

Abraham took them to the barn,
Showed them how he hayed Ruthie.
Let them pet her
And Hannah showed Abraham
She knew how to milk.

Now days Ruthie didn't have much milk
But it was enough for the kids
At least for a while.
Abraham split some firewood,
And they headed in for supper.

Supper done Hannah washed
Abraham and Issac dried.
They read the Bible for 30 minutes
And they were off to bed.

Abraham sat at the kitchen table
Shocked at how much he'd done.
How busy his day was,
He was glad for some time alone.

First chance he had to read his letter,
He was surprised he had waited so long.

Chapter 2

My Dear Abraham

I am understanding of your concern regarding your current predicament.
Though your reasoning is correct,
There is indeed an opportunity to grow,
To learn more the ways of our Lord.

I too, know self to be the largest single barrier
Preventing a Christian from turning
His complete life over to be guided by God.
A problem from the times of the Apostles.

Though I am not privy to the exact details of the situation,
I am excited for your opportunity to grow and learn
And I must admit
Hopeful to share in your discoveries
Concerning our Lord.

I have often felt I was on trial here on earth, just learning to grow
and deepen my relationship with our Lord
To be an example to others.

Egotistical no doubt,
But insight has changed my view.
Though I'm sure I'm the last one to realize
This is about no-one but my Lord and myself.

If I was the last resident of earth,
My job would still be the same.

*Deepen and broaden
my understanding of God's will.*

*From birth to death
HJ Foroon's life purpose is to be more Christ-like
Not selfish at all,
For the more Christ-like I become,
The more I am capable of loving and serving those
around me.*

*It is the self that creates the dilution,
That allows worldly clutter to interfere.
God's love
Increases my ability to love others.*

*Praying for your safety and growth
Your brother in Christ
HJ*

Chapter 3

Abraham looked in his shaving mirror,
He shaved occasionally
But rarely looked.
Brown eyes
Betsy said the color of chestnuts.

She used to pat that face,
Kiss that cheek.
Hard to believe you could get
That many furrows and creases
In such a small space.

That was forever ago,
When "I" was "we".
But Oh my sweet Betsy,
If you could only see what's in our guest room bed,
How your heart would sing.

Abraham was gonna need to find a church,
Children needed Church.
He reckoned he could school them.
So much to do.

Betsy had a cookbook in the old chest at the foot
of the bed,
He reckoned Issac and he
could weather Hannah's learning to cook.

Getting late and bed called,
But he felt a need to answer HJ's letter

The slightly stooped
Lean old figure,
Retrieved a pencil
And a piece of paper,

Then quietly slide out
The old kitchen chair,
Sat down at the table
Licked the pencil point and began.

Dear HJ

I yearn to speak of theology this evening,
Wax philosophical.
But I must admit to being kitchen-table bound,
Humbled by a missed black-eyed pea,

And over there a piece of carrot.
Both of which escaped an eleven year old's
attempt to clean up after supper.
Yet I still find myself pleased with her attempt,
Proud of her willingness.

It warms my heart to know she tried,
I applaud her trying,
I hope she found pride
In her effort.

It occurs to me
So must God view my failures.
My bumbled attempts at life.
I know Hannah will eventually grow
to be a better table cleaner.

And yet her process
Also contains value,
The wiping, either successful or not,
Each valued for the attempt as much as the success.

A child's first steps essential
To an adult's hundred-mile journey,
Equal value,
Equal success.

My attempts to listen to our Lord,
Are as valuable as when I hear Him completely.
I cannot berate the start of my journey,
And only praise my arrival.

To shame one's starting steps,
Curse ones stumbles,
Labels all learning
As missteps.

Does this reasoning not relegate failure to a sin?
Even if the attempt was honest?

After some Bible study
I was unable to find a
scripture condemning failure
(Perhaps you know of one)

So it is I, that condemns my failures,
It is I, that makes guilt of my attempts.
Surely the Lord must shake His head in dismay
As we His children load our backs with unearned guilt.

I feel privy to a new understanding with my Lord
For He has personally added to my studies, my learning
My books from "Beyond Good and Evil" The Screwtape
letters, Summa Theologiae, Christian Discourses,
Have been increased, enriched by two new lives, avenues
of learning,
the depth of which requires a lifetime to study.

Lord help me to look past,
To see through unselfish eyes
At the motive, the promise
To be more self-less.

Ah my distant friend
I will now lay down pencil
And give rest to an aging body,
For a new day of learning beckons.

Chapter 3

*I must remove the black eyed pea and carrot
My part in the clean up,
But I shall cherish their teachings.
Othello's crow will come early.*

Your brother in Christ

Abraham

Abraham's bed creaked comfortingly,
The house wasn't empty,
He wasn't alone.
The guest room no longer a guest room,
And sooner or later Issac would need a room
of his own.

Tomorrow they could discuss
Schooling and farm chores,
And maybe in a day or two, some fishing on
the creek.

There needs to be joy and laughter
Under these eaves,
And he had a feeling they could use some healing
For Hannah and Issac,
And yes maybe Abraham too.

As the days followed
There was learning,
Attempts,
Little to no recriminations,

Prayer and encouragement.

A laugh less rare,
And hope for more,
The art of smiling already grew
And broadened.

Saturday early,
Abraham found and cleaned
Betsy's old egg basket.
He had often teased her about its large size

Placing it on the kitchen table
He began filling it with biscuits,
Ham, fresh berries, butter, supplied by Ruthie
Some chicken he and Hannah had
Tried to fry last night.

Both Hannah and Issac had shed tears
when the chicken gave up its life for supper,
But agreed it tasted pretty good
for a first attempt at cooking.

The creek bank was a little chilly for Abraham
But the children didn't notice it.
Running, wading till their feet started turning blue
And they had to wrap Abraham's jacket around
them for warmth.

The sun did its job
And warmth grew,

Chapter 3

Full stomachs slowed them
And after a little quiet recovery time,

Leaning backs against a tree,
Hannah's head slid over against
Abraham's shoulder.
In a minute she sniffed and said

You smell like Abraham.
Abraham smiled and said "and what's that like?"
"Safe" Hannah said, "you smell like safe".

Monday brought a trip,
Books for schooling,
More clothes,
Supplies for bread baking.

Hope for a letter From HJ,
Maybe the two new books he'd ordered,
And Abraham would mail his latest letter to
his friend,
And maybe receive one.

The trip went well.
More giggling than before,
Tears when Issac banged his head,
Thoughts of a bag of sours balls quickly caused the
tears to dry.
Hannah ordered ingredients for an apple pie,
Went down the list of supplies,
Abraham left her the money to pay

And went next door to the Post Office.
HJ's and an Attorney's letters were waiting,
The book "The Children's Bible Reader"
Had arrived, but not "Bible stories".

Sitting on the bench in front of the store
Abraham read

Abraham my Friend!

Two children!
God must indeed
Look favorably upon you,
T'will surely vanquish loneliness.

I will not question a father's need
to abandon his children on a roadside,
It his path and for his discovery,
God can only be his judge.

As for the children, they have been truly blessed
To be found by Abraham Graham!
Christian, good man, Farmer, student,
Christian Philosopher,
And I'm proud to say, "my friend".

I must say upon receipt of your first letter
I felt myself in a wise teacher role,
Now after only a few letters,
I found myself joined by another sojourner.

Chapter 3

Trying to think as you.
I would have to say
We only learn,
When we are willing to be taught.
A student rather than a teacher am I now

For I, my dear friend,
am amazed at what you teach
Through your own
Christ-led learning experiences

I, having never being married,
Have no experience with wife
Nor children.
For the first time in my life
Do I realize my loss.

Surely a father,
If open-eyed and opened-hearted
Must be wiser,
For did not Jesus refer to God has his Father?

I know your quiet maybe damaged,
I know your time
Will no longer be for own,
But the rewards my dear Abraham
The rewards!

Blank slates (or mostly)
To be taught of the Lord's love,
To live a God-filled life,

Such an honor.

I pace in anticipation of
The arrival of your spirit-filled missives.
They are a cause for celebration
In my life.

I attend once a month
a group of Christian searchers such as we
I wondered if I could have your permission
To read your letters in the group?

I am always quoting you
And I think they would gain more enjoyment and insight
were you to allow me to use your exact words.

I understand if you would not agree to this.

Thank you again my dear friend
I await your next letter
Your friend
HJ

When he returned
The children were standing by the truck.
There was a tug at his heart
Longing for Betsy

For the words appeared in his head,
My Family,
It is Us,

Chapter 3

We Three.

The Children were tired going home
Abraham tried to drive on the grass when possible
So as not to jostle them as much while they
tried to sleep.
Hannah did not do well but Issac slept like a rock.

Tuesday was breakfast, chores
readings from the Screwtape letters,
reading from the New England Premier,
And reading and discussing the Bible.

After a busy week
And supper on Friday,
Hannah asked for a private moment
After Issac was in bed

They finished supper,
Hannah tucked Issac in,
Promised she would not be long
And went into the parlor.

She sat across from Abraham,
He could see in the lamp light
her eyes had welled up.
She said,"I don't think our pa is coming back from California".

Issac is very scared that we are going to have
to go away.

His birthday is on the 19th of December
And I was wondering,
If we worked very hard these next few weeks,
Could we stay until after his birthday?

Abraham excused himself,
Said he would return shortly,
And stepped into his bedroom,
Shocked and teary-eyed.

He had not cried since Betsy death.
Abraham had thought it, but not said it.
He had assumed they would stay forever
But he had not offered the children assurance.

He went back into the parlor
Where Hannah sat looking scared,
He asked her to wake Issac
And bring him in with her.

They came in
Issac looking sleepy and Hannah scared.
Abraham said "I have to apologize to you both,
I am sorry I have not asked you this sooner.

My wife Betsy died as you know
About ten years ago
Since then I have lived by myself,
Then I found two little people on the side
of the road.

Chapter 3

We have done a lot together
So now I would like to ask you,
Will you live with me forever?
Will you call this your home?

This will be your house
You won't ever have to leave.
I would like you to be my family
until you Pa comes back from California
to get you".

It would be hard to say
Who wept the most,
But that night changed a lot,
More than Abraham expected.

The next few days
Abraham thought he noticed more laughter.
Issac still only whispered in Hannah's ear,
But he smiled a lot, giggling often.

Tonight
No black-eyed pea vied for his attention,
No carrot piece caught his eye.
Abraham was heavy hearted

For he had come to a realization,
Humbled in prayer.
Abraham had to bow to God's will

A slightly stooped figure
Lanky in old age,
Walked a country kitchen floor,

Laid some paper down
On the table,
Pulled up a chair,
Licked his pencil point
And leaned over his paper
And wrote.

My Kind Friend HJ

That any would find my words interesting
Is but a testament to God
And naught to do with me,
Feel free to do as you will with my letters.

Today I ask for God's forgiveness,
I ask so you might bare witness
To my weakness.

While waxing philosophical
In my superior understanding
Of self and our Lord,
I succumbed to self
And lost the battle.

I am aghast,
Surprised by my exposure,
My egocentricity,

Chapter 3

I am still reeling.

I decided what to do with my children!
I knew why God placed them in my path,
I made plans for their future,
I was their savior,
I was their provider,
I was their guide.

It is evident
I have been boarded,
Taken without a shot.
"Self" stands undefeated
In my life.

None of these decisions,
Plans,
Were mine to make.
They were and are the Lord's children only.

He just loaned them to me
To be stewarded,
Fed, clothed,
Loved

And then await his guidance.
I asked for no guidance!

Today the young girl Hannah
Came to me
And asked,

When would I cast them out.

*When would I emulate
Their father's behavior?
I (self) was building their future
Without asking the Lord or them.*

*I reassured her of my intent
To love and protect them.
However
Only now do I see,*

*Only now do I realize
That also was self.
I made promise I might be asked to break,
It is all God's, our lives
The children and I.*

*I must now
Give them back,
Relinquish control
To God.*

The true owner.

*If he calls for me to cast them out once again,
I must
If he calls for me to find them new custodians,
I must*

Once again, I find I know nothing but God's love,

CHAPTER 3

The love of a father,
For a very selfish child.

I can only pray I have not damaged
These two tender souls.

Your humbled friend
Abraham

Early in the morning
Abraham called a parlor meeting,
Starting by saying
"It has come to my attention
That we have been neglecting
The most important member of our family".

Hannah and Issac looked a little confused
"God" Abraham said.
"I know we say our prayers
But we haven't, as a family,
Asked God to be a part of our family"

"Shall we do that right now?"
They both nodded vigorously
And then the group of three,
Kneeled on the parlor floor and bowed their heads.

"Lord we are three today asking
To be four,
Asking you to join us as our Father
and be our guide for this family.

Help us Lord
To have open ears, open eyes and open hearts.
To hear or see or feel your will,
to see the path you have chosen for us.

Hannah, Issac and Abraham
are here Lord
On our knees in the parlor,
We commit ourselves to You.

Chapter 4

The farm was different,
True, a little cleaner,
But more than that,
There was more color.

Those carefully spun, stall spider webs
Loaded with barn dust,
Waved comfortably
In the morning air.

The grass a brighter green,
The flaked red paint barn
shone scarlet
Against a deep blue Texas sky.

Othello with his feathered girls help,
Sheperded a group of fluffy pale yellow babies
Out of the coup, for a bug hunting lesson
On a cool December Texas morning.

Though Abraham had first feared
God's plans for Hannah and Isaac,
It only took prayer

To realize it was God's way
Not Abraham's.

God's wisdom for the future not
Abraham's human hopes and plans.
God's perfect guidance,
Not Abraham's incomplete and limited dreams.

It was not that God didn't care about
These dreams,
It was that He offered so much more.
Today safe in God's care
Abraham climbed the ladder,

He longed for his loft time,
But the climb was becoming
More difficult,
And coming back down dreaded.

Naught new in the loft except dust
And some fresh small footprints in old dust.
Too chilly now for a prolonged visit
But still the old chair and trunk
Tugged at is heart strings.

"Well my Lord
I seem to be full,
Completed,
An amazing wife, supporter, life-long friend
Now at rest with you.

Chapter 4

Two glorious, magnificent, children
You have given into my care
For Your time and Your reason
They are here.

I, Abraham Graham, your aged old servant,
Am awed and humbled by this honor.
I realize even more than ever
I must be on watch regarding my behavior,
My actions.

They will be copied into the lives of these two,
Far reaching,
Long lived new lights,
Burning brightly long after I'm gone.

Abraham climbed down
From the loft to find the children waiting.
They had discovered some old rope
In the feed room
And they asked if they could make a swing.

Abraham said they would start
first thing in the morning,
They laughed and skipped down the path to
the house,
Never such music had this farm heard!

After lunch
Abraham sat down to read the letter
From the attorney

He knew he had been avoiding it for a while,
But it was time.

Betsy's death had left Abraham
Owner of her mother and fathers
Old house and farmland
Two counties over.

The house had not been livable,
But the land, though having laid fallow,
Was good cleared farmland.
Abraham had written Mr R.L. Lansing Attorney at Law, Kingsley Texas
Asking if he knew of any interest in purchasing the old Sampson farm.

Mr Lansing was the Attorney that handled Betsy and her parent's wills.
Abraham knew that good farm-land could bring as much as $60 or more an acre,
But it wasn't easy to find a buyer.

The attorney went into detail about what was wrong with the farm,
And wrote that he could interest only one client,
And this client would pay only $23 dollars an acre for the 100 acres.

Abraham's heart sunk,
He had been financially comfortable
As one,

Chapter 4

But with the addition of 2 growing children,
His savings had been diminishing rather rapidly.

Well, he decided to pray about it
And turned to do some Bible reading.
Sitting in the parlor
He heard a truck coming up his road,
From the looks of it
It was Mr. Tilman.

Mr. Tilman was one of only a few farmers still
farming this area.
Abraham had bought some beef from him,
Some peaches too come to think of it.
Abraham walked to the front door
And saw Mr. Tilman walking up.

Mr. Tilman said "I were over'n Aspermont
This morning,
Don't know when t'was the last time I went
Over a year I'm sure.

This here feller at the Post Office asked if
I knew you,
I told him, yeah I did,
And he asked me if'n I drop a letter off to you,

I told him I would.
So here I am to give you this here letter"
And he searched his overalls bib pocket,
back pockets,

Looking kinda puzzled,

Turned went back over to his truck
He found the letter on the seat,
Brought back waving it in the air,
"I got it, I got it, I know'ed I had it, here ya'r,
right here".

Abraham thanked him,
Asked if he like to set a spell,
But Mr. Tilman said he had to get on home,
Waved goodbye,
And headed back up the road.

Unusual to get his letter from HR early
But he went in to read it.

My dear, dear friend,

Rarely am I speechless
This letter is no exception
But I must admit
your last letter has given me pause

Since you have not mentioned
Or acknowledged
The name connection of Abraham and Isaac until now,
I had refrained from bringing it up.

Your mentioning your possible sacrifice
Makes me feel I can broach the Subject.

Chapter 4

As you know
The biblical Abraham's hand was stayed,
You are a Godly man.
Perhaps your willingness to make the sacrifice will
be enough,
We know so little of God's plans.

In recent meetings, my friends I told you of
Brought up the names
Immediately after your eighth letter
Naming the children.

I know I mentioned my meetings
A core group of seven of us meet once a month
Very informal,
In the basement of the Fort Worth Calvary Church.

Reverend Stewart, pastor of Fort Worth Calvary, Dr.
Edgar Rainer, Department Head of Theology, South
Western Baptist Theological Seminary, Father Liam
McAnderson, Rector of The Church of St Thomas, William
Franklin, Department Head of The School of Educational
Ministries, South Western Seminary, Reverend Horace
Dobkins, Trinity Methodist Church, Reverend Samuel
P. Framton, Pastor, Bethal Lutheran Church, and your
humble servant and friend
Heed J. Foroon Jr

From all the titles and degrees, you would not recognize
these humble men
True lovers of the Lord searchers for the truth.

All my dear Abraham, admirers of yours.
Your simple insights seem to cut through to the heart of the matter.
You have become our eighth member.

You. my friend have sparked some heated debates and changed or enriched thinking.

We all pray for you

Your friend
HR

Abraham sat for a while
Letter in his hand
Not sure what he felt
He guessed, pleased that the men

Found his letter noteworthy.
However disconnected,
He only wrote what he thought,
What he experienced,
what he felt God revealed.

God was surely the one of note.
The Lords wisdom,
The Lords plans.
A signpost won't take you to town,
It just points the way.
Abraham Graham, the signpost.

Chapter 4

Supper needed to be made,
Hannah and Isaac were still outside playing,
They deserved it they had worked hard,
And soon the weather would keep them inside.

Abraham cut up some potatoes,
Open a jar of crowder peas he had put up earlier
And cut some generous slabs off ham
For two hungry kids.

Almost as soon as the cooking was done,
They came running through the back door
Full of giggles and laughter
Nearly out of breath.

Abraham felt he should applaud,
He stood in awe.
Look at what God has wrought,
A concert of childish joy,

And he as audience.
Abraham Graham as witness to God's masterpiece.
Music, bells, chimes, freshness, excitement innocence
Sparkling. Thank you with all I am Lord Jesus
to be allowed this late in life, to witness
this wonder.

Hannah's face fell suddenly when she realized she
was late for cooking
Becoming almost fearful,

Abraham stood them in front of him
And said,

"I want to thank you both
For your laughter, your joy in playing,
For your hard work with your chores
For your living with me,

But most of all tonight thank you Hannah for letting me cook for you two
I do enjoy it,
It allowed me to feel I was giving you a little something.
Though you are turning into a better cook than I,
We are finishing up your biscuits from
this morning."

The guilt fell from Hannah's face
And the laughter returned.
Soon finished and as the table was cleared
Abraham received a hug from Hannah.

As they were both drying their hands
Isaac said in a loud voice
"Hannah makes the best biscuits!"
Abraham and Hannah stared open mouthed
Isaac's first above a whisper words!

It was past 8:00 the children were tucked in,
The kitchen table was cleared and dishes washed.

Chapter 4

Abraham took his pencil and paper
And reached out to his friend

My HJ

The august company you keep!
I am envious of your meetings,
The wisdom to be gathered
But in all honesty,

I have more than I deserve here.
Today the children came running through the back door
Full of giggles and laughter
Nearly out of breath

I felt I should applaud!
I stood in awe!
Look at what God has wrought
A concert of childish joy,

And I the single audience.
Abraham Graham as witness to God's masterpieces,
Music, bells, freshness, excitement
Innocence.
Do all parents know?
Do all grandparents that witness this joy applaud?

Oh, I so wish for Betsy
At moments like this,
But I know so well
She knows more,

Just being in the presence of the Lord.

I believe it is my task
As a child of God
To be aware,
More and more

I feel my only reason on earth
Is to learn of the Lord,
To follow in His ways.
All else is superfluous.

It is like the static on my radio,
In the way,
Cluttering,
Clouding my view of the Lord.

Is worship church hymns?
Sermons?
We are right now too far from a church
So we gather in the parlor
Hold hands and pray.

We read a scripture,
Talk about what we think it means,
We talk about when and where we saw God
In the past week.

What we might have done to please God more,
We try each one, to tell God how important to us He is,
We finish with a promise prayer saying,

Chapter 4

what we hope to do for God in the coming week.

Abraham, Hannah and Isaac's Church service

We always sing Jesus Loves me, every week

*I am full to overflowing
Blinded by so much to see,
My head is filled with this new realization.*

*God is so good to me!
And I thank you for letting me share*

*I do value our friendship so,
And envy your meetings.*

*Your humble admirer
Abraham*

Next morning
After chores and reading,
Isaac was the tree climber
With a ball of string.

Pulling rope up into the old barn Oak,
learning to use a brace and bit.
There were knots and boards,
And gleeful screams were soon heard
As toes pointed skyward.

This new week brought their trip to town.

No letter to look forward to
With it being delivered,
But there were supplies to pick up.

Abraham was not sure where the money was going
to come from in the future
However, since relinquishing ownership of
the children,
Abraham had to give up concern over their
well being
They now belong completely to God.

Abraham could only do what he could,
The rest was in the Lord's hands.
So the trip would be carefree
With a little work.

He visited with Apermont's town Marshall
While the children spent their nickel
each on candy,
Not seeming to notice the reduction in
candy money.

The Marshal told Abraham
he had a sister lived over near Kingsley,
Said her and her husband were well-to-do farmers.
Said he'd tell'em 'bout the Sampson farm,
Next time he wrote.
Abraham didn't put much pay in it
But it added to their conversation.

Chapter 4

He said no one had been asking about the children,
Figured they were Abraham's long as he wanted
'um around.
Marshall got a might choked on his chaw
And Abraham saw the children at the truck,

So they loaded up and headed back.
Isaac was talking more, louder
Seems like he was improving every day.
His Birthday had passed,
And they had put up a Christmas tree,
But neither Hannah or Isaac seemed interested.

So tonight Abraham had bought something special.
Popcorn, tinsel
A pocketknife for Isaac,
Some hair ribbons,
And a silver hairbrush and mirror.

They weren't real silver but they looked like it
The set cost $2.59 and the Knife $1.69
More than they could afford,
But far less than they deserved.

They made popcorn balls,
Lit candles,
Threw tinsel on the tree.
Hannah said the firelight made the tree dance
with the tinsel on it.

Othello was late this Christmas morn,

It was frosty outside
So Abraham dressed quickly
to make a fire in the kitchen,

Only to find Hannah
With a huge smile,
Wearing one of Betsy's aprons
Standing in the warm kitchen,
Biscuits baking.

Abraham laughed out loud
"Well, well! Would you look at Miss Hannah
Up before me fresh baked biscuits,
Eggs and bacon cooking
What a great Christmas morning!

I don't know what to say
You've already made Christmas special
Lets wake Isaac!"
They went in and shook Isaac awake.

It was a great breakfast
And after they were full
Abraham took them to the parlor,
With the heat of the kitchen
and freshly lit parlor stove they were warm.

They read the story of Jesus's birth,
Sang Silent Night and Oh come all ye faithful.
After they finished Abraham handed each child
their present.

CHAPTER 4

Isaac's eye got big as saucers,
Quickly ripping away the paper
He turned the pocketknife over and over
Staring at it in disbelief.

Hannah sat,
She did not open hers,
She held them in her lap
Touching them gently,
Smiling and watching Isaac.

"Well Hannah
We're waiting
Open you presents
Show us"
Abraham said.

She lowered her eyes and shook her
Head.
Abraham said "is there something wrong
Are you unhappy?"

Her eyes gave her away again
As they welled up.
She dropped her head
And shook it side to side,

"I can't, I just can't open them,
If I do it will all be over.
I have wanted this to happen my whole life,
If I open them now it will all end."

Abraham rose and went over and sat beside her on
the settee,
Put his arm around her and said,
"It won't end darlin',
this is just the beginning.

It's the start of your new life,
Trust the Lord to love and take care of you,
Show Isaac and I what you have."

Hannah slowly methodically removed
Bows, untied ribbons unfolded the paper
And stared,
They could not have been more special if
they'd been made of real silver or even gold.

She cried and touched them gently
over and over
Saying "Oh, Oh"

For dinner
They had roast chicken,
Sweet potatoes, corn Abraham had put up
early fall,
Biscuits
And a blackberry pie.

Hannah truly was learning to cook.
Then Isaac had to have some alum on his finger
and a bandage tied around it.
The carving would now have to wait

until the bandage didn't get in the way
of holding his new knife.

Abraham
Was by far the most blessed.
The most full spirituality,
Blessed beyond his imagination

Oh my Lord Jehovah
I am not worthy!"

Chapter 5

Not all of Abraham's life
Was turmoil
Upheaval was not always present
He treasured the mundane

Quiet time though rare was there
Reading
Studying
And the all important
Listening to God

Abraham had no doubts
Issac now a loud seven year old
And a soon to be thirteen Hannah
Were treasures

Sure there were tears, temper flares
All a part of learning
Abraham could usually find a
Bible scripture to fit the situation

They always read it together
Prayed together

Abraham never forced them!
God and the Bible were always used
As support, reinforcements

It was becoming time to get Issac his own room
A twelve year old young lady needs her privacy
Based on the house size
There was only part of the back porch

The front door opened from the front porch into
the parlor
The guest room was to the right

Back half of the house
The kitchen was on the left, Abraham's bedroom
was on the right

The left half of the back porch
Now used for stacking firewood
Out of the weather
And the right half was near the well
So it was where their washstand was set up

Seems smartest to build a shed close by
to keep the fire wood dry
Then close in the left half
of the back porch

There would be more than enough room
for a young boy
With a little moving around

Chapter 5

They could make a door off the kitchen

Breakfast and chores finished
Study's done
The firewood shed was built by dark
Hannah and Issac both were
Excited about building Issac
His own bedroom

Friday by dusk the door was cut
The room closed in
All day Saturday
They worked on getting it ready

Issac slept
With the door open
For the first night
in his own room

Abraham Hannah and Issac
Knelling in the parlor
Thanked the lord
For the new room

It was a time of peace
On the Graham farm
Often the chance to worry appeared
As Abraham watched their savings diminish

But prayer and thanksgiving
Soon healed

Maybe it was Hannah's laughter
Or maybe just noticing less cut fingers
from Issac and his whittling

Monday's trip this month brought
HJ's letter
Along what seemed to be a a monthly talk with
the Marshall
A reasonably pleasant man
So it was not unwelcome

The Marshall commented on the manners of the
two children
Their joy and cheerfulness
"Them kids of your'n are happy as a couple
a puppies"

Abraham agreed
But treasured most "those kids a your'n"
He knew they we're property of the Lord's
But the joy of the loaning was overwhelming

The Marshall said he had visited his sister
this past week
He told her about the Sampson farm
She said she tell folks

It was dry enough to drive beside the ruts
so Issac and Hannah were able to nap going home
Lunch finished, time for study
And time for Abraham to read HJ's letter

My Friend Abraham

If one can't be honest with his friends
Then he has no friends
Please forgive my honesty
I do not mean to burden you

I know this will pass
I just am feeling distant from the Lord
A poor Christian
Unworthy

It seems so simple
"Jesus said unto him,
Thou shalt love the Lord thy God with all thy heart,
and with all thy soul, and with all thy mind."

If we were able to do this faithfully
There would be no confusion
No questions
Perhaps even no sin

I never doubt the Lord,
But I forget.
I get busy with the minutiae
The insignificant

I allow the worry of living
To crowd out the joy of living
I permit the difficulty of drawing a breath
To shroud the privilege of breathing

I am owed naught!
Earned naught
It by the Lord's grace I am!
I am, by His blessing only

And yet I take my eyes off the Lord
I forget to whom I owe my breath
I ignore the author of my laughter
The pacifier of my troubled soul

I am appalled at my ungratefulness
My callousness
I forget
I do all these things

Only to turn by habit
To thank God for my food,
To visit Him in a house of worship in Sunday's
I am but an Ingrate, a charlatan

I don't know the answer
Why am I uninspired
Deaf, dumb,
And blind

Forgive my lament
My soul's whimper

I am well
Just discouraged

Chapter 5

Yours in Christ
HJ

Abraham felt for his friend
It had been a while since he
Had been so attacked
But you are never immune

He thought during the day
Of his friend under attack
The darkness of these attacks
Are still vivid memories

Abraham was sure all Christians
Suffered these attacks at one time or another
He found a moment sat at the kitchen table
Stared at his blank paper
Then licking his pencil point wrote

My Dear HJ

Ah my friend!
Rarely a topic of conversation between us
We have forgotten to speak of Satan
But my HJ he has not forgotten us

He would admit your being a Christian
But question your dedication
He would agree with your salvation
But question your loyalty

King of the half truths
Lord of yes buts
Your love of the Lord
Troubles him deeply

We must expect attacks
Prepare for temptations
"Put on the whole armor of God,
that ye may be able to stand against the wiles of the devil."

Fear not my dear friend
These feelings we all know too well
That's why we are considered children,
The human plight

God never has to prove His
Presence
He Is
Never has to show His self
For He is never hidden

It is we,
His children.
Our fears calling for more
Our weaknesses struggling for support

We often question
"What do we do when God is silent"
When our prayers go unheard
Unanswered

Chapter 5

Poppycock, balderdash
We are NEVER unheard!
We are NEVER unanswered!
It is often not what we asked for
When we wanted it

The answer is always there,
Always the right one,
Always best for us,
Always Gods will.

When we don't see what we asked for
Don't hear what we wanted to hear
We assume He hasn't answered.
It is up to us to accept the answer

When we pray for an egg out of hunger
The hen pecks the bug
Then begins the process of laying
While we turn to say
See! No egg

Fear not my friend HR

God forgives all when asked
He loves us with a father's patience
We have been saved by His Son
All is well in Christ our Lord

You will be in our prayers

Abraham
Current guardian,
And student of
Hannah and Issac
And our Lord

It was a cold January
Abraham had been busy
Chopping fire wood
Even with Issac and Hannah's help

It was getting farther from the house
And more difficult to pull
To add to their expenses
They needed a horse or mule

To pull the firewood from the woods
Over a mile away
It took the three of them hours
And were left generally exhausted

Monday on the way to town
They stopped by Mr Tilman's
The farm down the road
To see if he had any old horses or mules

Tilman said
Can't keep an animal that can't earn their keep
Work til they can't
Then their fed to the hogs

CHAPTER 5

Old widow Wilson's
Got an ancient old mule
She can't seem to let it die
But she might sell it

So on down the road the find widow
Wilson
They soon closed the deal
And Hannah Issac and Abraham
Owned a 32 year old mule
Jeroboam tall boney lanky
They had to promise the Widow Wilson
To take care of him

They walked him back to the farm
Jeroboam took their Monday town trip
so they set out Tuesday
For supplies and mail

While Hannah and Issac spent their nickels
Abraham sat near the pot bellied stove in the
mercantile
To read his letter from HJ

My Abraham

I cling to your letter
As a drowning man
To a floating cask
A starving man to a scrap of bread

These words the Lord sent me
From your pencil
From farm worn hands
Hands that sowed
Hands the harvested

Abraham reader of Jean Paul Sartre,
Nietzsche,
Reached out with a wisdom
far greater than his own

And reminded me
It's a Joy to be A Child of God
To be redeemed promised eternal life
Protected by He who watches the sparrow

Nourished by he that cares
for the lilies of the field
I Heed J Foroon belong solely
to the Great Jehovah

Strange how we are lulled
Sung songs of lies
Turned ever so slowly
Away from our Lord

Think not of Satan
False profit of doom
Look away from he of the shadows
Stop your ears to dark whispers

Chapter 5

The great deceiver
Father of lies
Sower of half truths
Serpent of the abyss

I am delivered
Blessed exonerated
Liberated
Thank you for you reminder

Oh my dear friend
If I could shake your hand
T'would be such and honor
Maybe one day

Your true friend and admirer
HJ

It was one thing to praise God
Speaking of His wonders
Expressing his awe in the Lords
Love, vastness, compassion
And so much more

Having somebody speak in glowing terms about
himself was another
It was uncomfortable
He was glad HJ saw through the wiles of the devil

As they left Aspermont
The black skies opened up

Spit rain and sleet down
On the little farm truck

Slipping and sliding
The truck struggled in and out of
The ruts
Some sleet and rain made it way into the cab
Hannah and Issac
Wrapped in a blanket
Cuddle up on the seat
And slid up against Abraham

A one hour trip
Took over two
But they arrived safe
Running inside to light fires and lamps

Home
Thank you Lord for reminding us
Of the joys of dry warm clothes
And a comforting fire

The children dosed in the parlor
by the fire
As Abraham sat at the table pencil in hand
Licked the pencil point and began

Mr Dear HJ
A face to face visit would be a great thing
Indeed.

Chapter 5

But I deserve no accolades
I am a planter of seeds
I reap what Gods returns to me at harvest
No more

I love the earth
Rich deep soil
To watch it curl and roll
Split by my double shovel

To watch the rows
Green in spring
Leap upwards
And reach for the sky

To hear the whispering grain
As it ripples in wind waves
Or the rustle of cornstalks
Dancing in a breeze

I am in awe of my Lords gifts
The deep joy I've been given
The satisfaction
And peace

I read because I admire
I read because I want to know more
About who loves me so, about who I love
And who sacrificed His son for me

Not for wisdom
No acclaim
But to love Him more
Accept Him unreservedly

Any honest man
Would know
He was not worth redemption
Except by a father's love

A tremendous Father
Capable of infinite forgiveness
Patience
Understanding

I have seen satan
In the corn blight
A spring drought
A cloud of grasshoppers so large
They blackened the sky

I've heard his whisper
In my ear
You need God
You need rain
If He really loved you
Those pigs wouldn't have died
Sure there's a God
He just doesn't care about you

Chapter 5

I refuse to hear him any more
My weapon of choice
Love
I love my Lord

I thank Him continually
By joyful noise
With my favorite hymns
I believe satan runs
when faced with a heart for God
Singing "Oh How I Love Jesus"

I am so glad
you have found your joy once more

Romans 15:13
May the God of hope fill you with all joy and peace as you trust in him, so that you may overflow with hope by the power of the Holy Spirit.
Your brother in Christ

Abraham

That night as sleet and rain
Rattled farm house windows
Abraham
Hannah and Issac

Slept snug and warm
As did Ruthie, the feathered girls
Family of pigs and of course

Jeroboam
With a little extra oats
As promised to widow Wilson

Chapter 6

There was frost on the inside
Of Abraham's bedroom window,
He slipped his freshly washed shirt
over his head,

Slid his long-john clad legs
into his clean overalls,
Stuck a bandana
In the bib pocket.

Woolen socks took the bite out of cold brogans,
He filled his back pockets from the top
Of Betsy's old dresser,
Headed for the kitchen.

Lit the coal-oil lamp,
Quickly stuck a match to the kindling,
Slid the coffee pot onto the eye,
Headed for the back door.

The early morning trip to the outhouse
Was bitter.
Both children used the slop jars,

But often had to be reminded
To empty and rinse them in the morning.

Breakfast followed
Then the children did their chores,
While Abraham went to talk with Jeroboam
Tall, peaceful, hungry
Aged white muzzle.

He was a healthy old fellow.
All they needed was some help
Hauling wood,
He wouldn't even notice the load.

Jeroboam nuzzled Abraham's hand full of oats,
Snorting, waving ears,
Listening to Abraham's soft low voice.
Jeroboam was comfortable.

Abraham's mind was troubled,
He trusted God implicitly,
But his saving was dwindling rapidly,
Challenging his financially cautious nature.

He returned to the warmth of the kitchen
For a Hannah cooked breakfast,
A three person clean up,
And everyone went their own way

Abraham sat at the table,
One more cup of coffee,

Chapter 6

Listening to the children talking and studying
In the parlor.

Abraham felt the need to write HJ again,
Maybe it was just to gather his thoughts.
Whatever the reason
He sharpened his new pencil,
And licked the point.

HJ my friend

True faith

It is a fight for me.
I can logically and faithfully tell you
God will provide,
And I believe it.

But then I worry,
And worry only comes from lack of faith.
If I truly believed
I would not worry.

What often appears as child like oblivion
In some,
Is really complete faith,
Absence of doubt.

We sinners interpret complete faith
As idiocy or complete lack of caring,
Thinking if you don't worry

You don't care.

Surely complete trust in God
Negates fear.
Faith
Will make worry pointless.

The Mimosa tree out side my kitchen window
Taps in the winter wind,
The farm looks bleak.
Funny how we choose what we see.

If I look for green,
The winter is dark austere.
If I am looking for snow-scapes,
Warm fires, sparkling frosty mornings,
Winter is beautiful.

I work to choose the light,
To choose the joy,
To choose the love,
I often fail.

I would chase this faith,
I would fight against doubt,
I would turn my back on worry,
I would cast out the "what if's".

Each a insurmountable task
But I will continue to try,
I am most certainly blessed

Chapter 6

Beyond my deserving.

I hope Joy resides with you this day.

God's humble servant
Abraham

Abraham's life was governed by what he expected
He was looking for God's blessings,
Therefore they were everywhere.

Jeroboam pulled wood.
Casually,
He sauntered,
No load for this old fellow!

One or two trips a day
Were no problem.
Especially with the oats, brushings
And occasional carrots and apples.

The firewood shed was soon filled to overflowing,
Studies were going well,
And the monthly Aspermont trip
Was next Monday.

It was a "Sir Walter Raleigh" tobacco can,
Abraham's bank.
Abraham's budget by himself had
Run about $8 to $12 per month.

Current expenses had doubled or occasion-
ally tripled,
The bank was shrinking.
Abraham reminded himself
That God knew.

God will provide,
Have no fear
Such a simple thing,
To be so hard.

Hannah and Isaac have not asked,
Do we have enough money.
They believe without doubt
Abraham will take care of them.

Abraham, older and wiser,
Worries that his Father
Doesn't have enough money,
Or will let him be poor.

Who is the wiser?
Who the stronger person of faith?
Abraham cherished that trust,
As God would cherish Abraham's faith.

The three spent their Sunday in worship
Hannah and Isaac were full of questions about God
and the Bible.
They then went to bed early
In anticipation of their trip to town.

Chapter 6

Bright and cold morning but full of a hot breakfast
They bundled up
Brought extra blankets,
And headed for town.

Abraham had a special reason for leaving' early,
They stopped by the Tilman place
So Abraham could talk to Mrs Tilman.

Ester Tilman raised a brood of eight
3 boys and 5 girls
Abraham asked if she would visit with Hannah
Explain women's happenings to her,
She said she'd love to sometime next week.

Abraham also asked if she could make a
list of goods,
a soon to be thirteen years old girl,
would need in the way of petticoats and other
paraphernalia
He figured to get it this trip.

Mrs Tillman was very kind and
They arranged for Hannah to come
By for a crochet lesson early Wednesday afternoon,
Hannah was excited.

Aspermont was busy
The counter lady in the mercantile
Was helping Hannah with Mrs Tilman's list,

Isaac stared at the candy counter and two new
Benjamin Pellet guns.

The Marshall came by to pass the time.
Finally Abraham made his visit to the post office
A letter from HJ, and a letter from
A R.W. Lipton attorney at law from Roby,
Fisher County.

Once again by the mercantile potbelly stove,
Abraham helped himself to a rocking chair, and a free cracker and cheese
First the letter from Betsy's folk's county.

It was an answer from God!
An attorney from Sweetwater,
Representing a farmer of Nolan county,
Married to a certain Aspermont Marshall's sister

Made a firm offer of $61 dollars an acre.
Here it was, financial security.
With awe, love and a few tears
He begged the Lord to forgive his fear and doubt.

Abraham borrowed a piece of paper, envelope and pencil
He responded immediately to the attorney accepting the offer
Requesting all papers to be sent to Aspermont.

Chapter 6

Then with a few minutes left as Hannah finished her shopping
Abraham turned to HJ's letter
Always so important

Dear Abraham

I must admit to being cloistered,
Cushioned,
Surrounded by my Christian friends.
I am rarely attacked
By unbelievers.

Rarely forced to defend my faith
Never threatened by financial difficulties,
My books sales continue to sustain me
A retirement home furnished by my denomination
coddles me.

Yet emptiness tugs at my faith,
Time to spare can lead me into doubt.
I sat and stared today
Breakfast finished,

Your letter in hand
My eyes were focused on the treetops
The ones lining Belmont Avenue.
Unclad weaving of branches and twigs

All in waiting for the next spring.
The horny toads

So common on our grounds,
Are in hibernation waiting for that day,

Yet the plight of the Christian is different.
We also wait
Indeed for a new spring,
A returning of the Lord.

Yet we do not lie dormant while waiting,
We are allowed this time for
Study reflection,
For experiences to strengthen our faith,
And also trial and error.

Your letters are a window,
A view of another world.
Your realizations exciting for me
Your revelations valuable to my growth.

I take it all in,
I pray more and more.
We have daily church services here
I am feeling closer and closer to God.

So today
I will listen, learn,
And act for God
In every part of my life.

I am praying for you, Hannah, and Isaac
What a blessed place the Graham farm is.

Chapter 6

A fitting memorial for Betsy Graham
A beacon for the Lord.

Your fellow Christian
Waiting on the Lord
HJ

Abraham stared at the belly of the stove
Stained
Glowing a black red with heat.

There's a warmth also in the smell of soot
and firewood,
A reassurance of safety from the cold.
A heart string tempter when forced to think of the cold truck ride home.

Sending the children to the truck
Abraham got the secret special package he had ordered for Hannah,
And a package of coco powder, and a can of
Postum, a new hot drink Mrs Abrams said was good

It was his companions that eased the trip,
Blanket wrapped and curled up next to him
for warmth
Tired from trip and excitement ,
And home always was welcoming.

Abraham's mind was racing
$6100

This would ease his fears.
So amazed at the ways of the Lord.

He felt they would need a new milk cow soon,
Poor Ruthie was just not giving
Much milk any more.
Growing children needed milk.

Hannah's cooking was becoming
Much better,
Her biscuits most of the time turned out great
Eggs good,
Bread she was working on.

Isaac had taken Abraham's
4-10 single barrel shotgun
And killed a rabbit.
When Abraham
Reached him, he was sitting by the rabbit crying.

Abraham sat on the ground beside him put his arm around him
Until he finished.
Then said "I'm glad you were sad the rabbit died,
But I also want you to be proud.

You have supplied Hannah, you and I with a grand supper,
You are a fine hunter,
Who respects his prey,
Killing anything should never be a casual thing.

Chapter 6

They walked back to the house
Isaac watched as Abraham
Prepared the rabbit
And Hannah fried as she had learned to
fry chicken.

A fine meal,
Isaac was not quite as sad when Abraham
and Hannah
Thanked him for supplying a fine supper.

As the children turned in
Abraham sat at the Kitchen table.

My Dear HJ

I again have
Found myself rediscovering the wheel,
Reinventing fire
Rather than learning from those
Far wiser than I.

Many brilliant Christ inspired
Men and women
Have put pen to paper
With heart-felt answers and revelations.

The Bible tells
Over and over
Of God's love,
A desire to help His children

I have read His promises.
I have heard great theologians
Discuss God's steadfastness,
But as the deaf, I did not listen with my heart.

I know me and my impurities,
My failings, weaknesses,
But I know I am redeemed,
Saved,
A Child of God.

However I still stand in awe
Of the true perfection of our Lord,
The example,
The one True Love.

Even though I have failed the Lord
Often proven false,
Doubted His Love
And caring,

He remains faithful,
Keeps to His word,
For I, as the flowers of the field,
Have been suppled.
As I wandered,
Thought, questioned, doubted,
God continued
My care.

Needless to say the children and my

Chapter 6

Financial future is now secure.
God supplied
All glory to His name.

I regret my worry,
My fear,
Trepidation,
I ask for His forgiveness.

And I so enjoy receiving your letters.

I do envy your time to spend
In study,
With nothing but pursuit of God's truth
as your daily goal

Such a simple thought,
The winter of life, as our school
Time, to grow
Before the coming of the Lord.

Though I must say
God's gift of this life of mine
Is beyond my understanding,
A mystery to me.

We are indeed in waiting,
And like the apostles
In Gethsemane
We often find ourselves spiritually asleep.

More and more I realize I know less and less.

Thank you for your friendship

Abraham

That next morning after breakfast
Was Hannah's visit with Mrs Tilman.
Isaac and Abraham left to themselves
started planning Hannah's birthday,
About 10 days away

Abraham had bought a fancy dress,
A shawl to match,
And a Bible with her name on the cover.
He laid them out for Isaac to pick
Which he'd like to give to Hannah as his present.

Isaac chose the dress.
Soon they had three packages wrapped
Tied with twine,
And hidden in Abraham's chifforobe.

Isaac was sworn to secrecy
And they headed back to pick up Hannah.
Mrs Tilman had given her a lot of recipes
Some extra crochet yarn
She talked about how kind Mrs Tilman was.

Hannah's birthday morning,
They sat her down washed breakfast dishes,

Chapter 6

Cleaned the kitchen
Then took her to the parlor.

They had her close her eyes
While they placed her three presents
In her lap.
Then when she opened her eyes they sang
Happy birthday

To their surprise Hannah burst into tears
They stared at each other,
After a little while
Hannah said "I've never been so happy"

Abraham and Isaac were happy too.

Chapter 7

Abraham watched
Two small heads,
Bent over their books
Intently reading.

He had to remind himself
Whose children they are.
God's children,
Abraham but the caretaker.

Instead of feeling proud
As if he had anything to do with it,
He stood in the door,
Watched,
And praised God.

"You are an amazing Father
To care for these children,
To nourish and protect them
To love them so."

"Lord you are an awesome Father
To bless Your servant Abraham this greatly,

To allow him be a tiny part of Your great plan
For these two precious souls."

Never had Abraham been so happy,
At least not since Betsy passed.
A new type of love
A new life.

Studies finished, he heard the beginnings
of laughter.
They both put their assigned book reports
on the table by Abraham's arm.
Isaac grabbed his coat and headed for the barn.

Hannah was going to try a new
Bread recipe,
It was one Mrs Tilman gave her.
Hannah was halfway through
A throw she was crocheting.

The change was visible,
Less timid, self assured,
Mrs Tilman was working miracles
only a mother can for a girl.

Abraham read the reports,
And was of course was impressed with both,
And then started his list
For their Aspermont trip tomorrow.

CHAPTER 7

Evenings were fun,
They listened to a radio show,
When reception was good,
Then Abraham read from the Bible,

Often causing droopy eyes.
The children had asked
If they could hug his neck before bed,
And it immediately became a treasured ritual.

Monday morning brought a cold north wind
Extra blankets and bundling up as
They headed for Aspermont.
While in the mercantile the snow started,

From the Mercantile windows it was a beautiful sight.
The giant pot bellied stove poured out heat,
The air thick with the smells of fresh
Smoked bacon,
Spices, new denim overalls.

Abraham had to rush the children,
For he knew the driving home
Would be more difficult in the snow.
Soon letter in pocket, supples bundled up, they set off towards home.

At first it was beautiful and fun,
But the snow thickened quickly
Blanketing the roads and making it hard to see.

Isaac and Hannah's wonder started
Turning to fear and worry.

Slow driving and wandering off the road a little,
It was almost 3 hours after leaving Aspermont
Before the old fence and gate told them they were almost home.

They lit parlor fire and kitchen stove,
The heat soon brought cheer.
Some popcorn and coco,
And the snow was once more
Beautiful.

Isaac was worried though,
He was fretting over Jeroboam.
All of Abraham assurances
In vain,
Isaac insisted on a trip to the barn.

Touched by the loving concern of the now
eight year old
Isaac and Abraham bundled up,
Lit a lantern and plowed through the snow
To the barn.

A carrot and a couple of handfuls of oats for the ancient mule
And they reappeared at the kitchen door,
Stomping and shaking off snow. Hannah pretended to fuss

Chapter 7

Over the mess in "her" kitchen.

Eyes soon grew heavy
Prayers said, Bible read,
Hugs exchanged,
And the Graham house settled down
For a snowy sleep.

Abraham pulled the chair up to the table,
Saw a small piece of biscuit
Over-looked against the butter dish.
And smiled thinking of a missed black eyed pea
and a piece of carrot

He tenderly opened his letter and read.

My dear Abraham

I know well
The pursuit of the known.

Pursuit of understanding,
Thirst for reasons,
A map of the future
Naught to be ashamed of.
Even though mapped by another

I think most have to find out for ourselves
That the stove is indeed hot,
That you may indeed slip into the puddle,
And yes our Lord does remain faithful,

Even when we stumble and fall.

So my friend the re-explorer
Lament not,
Throw off the cloak of self recrimination,
For I see another you!

I am not sure you the explorer
Are not eclipsed
By the ability of you the grower.
To raise from the ground new life,

Tiny seeds to fields of grain,
Acres of corn and beans,
A farmer, the noblest trade.
what could be more rewarding?

No doubt at the mercy of God,
The weather,
The insects,
All beyond your control

With only prayer and faith
As your finishing tools.
When all else is done
It is given into the hands of God.

And now you teach.
Perhaps the reasons for your study
all these years,
All your experiences.

Chapter 7

My dear, Abraham
Not just for God's two lambs,
For we seven in Fort Worth,
Read and learn as well.

Farmer,
Student of God,
Teacher,
Father,

We spoke in length
Regarding you and your last letter.

The group have been meeting
the last two months here in our lounge.
Due to my recent lack of mobility of late
They are fine Christian men.

I insisted they meet without me,
But they would have none of it.
They arranged for the use of our lounge
and surprised me.

Such a kind and tender gesture ,
I am flattered
as well as touched.
We await your next letter

So my wise friend
Write when you can

Honored to be your friend I remain
HJ

Decreased mobility!
Concerned about his friend
Abraham was slow to fall asleep.
His bed springs sang a sleepless song
Of tossing and turning.

It was also bright outside
The light through his window
throwing shadows on his ceiling,
The moon reflected back by acres of snow.

He laid in bed
Snug under his quilts
And lulled himself to sleep
By counting his blessings.

Far two many
To numerous to count,
Abraham had decided years earlier
Not to wait to be"tempest tossed"
But to give all worry and fear to his Father.

Abraham slowly drifted into a deep sleep
It had been quite a day.

After what seemed like only a short time
The household heard the somewhat muffled cry
of Othello,

Chapter 7

Giving his "staying in-house" sun calling,
For Othello was no fan of the snow.

Aah! But the sun must come up!

Boiling coffee, sizzling bacon and eggs
Big fluffy biscuits
Changed lives, brightened mornings.
Soon tousled heads, sleepy eyes
Gave way to strawberry jam grins.

Early fast trips to the out house
A quick feeding,
Trip to the barn for Ruthie, Jeroboam
Othello and his ladies,
And the three snuggled in for studies
And letter writing.

My Friend H.J.

I am concerned about your limited mobility.
What is the prognosis my friend?
Often what one fears of the unknown
can be greater than the truth.
Please let me know.

I always found my farming fulfilling,
Often found joy in the harvest
Never wished to do anything else,
However I've come to realize I occupy these acres
Not own them.

True, I held an earthly piece of paper claiming ownership,
But in a hundred years no one will know
I plowed this ground,
Harvested these fields,
My name was never on this land.

These two new fields I tend
For what ever time God allows,
They are different
Grander, longer lasting.

For all my "tending"
Will shape these lives,
Their children's lives
Their children's children's lives.

Idea's are far flung seeds
Something said casually,
A careless action,
Can influence a generation,
Mold future lives.

"Lord Jesus guide my tongue,
Guard my footsteps that I might not
Unknowingly mislead another by
Poor example or word".

Christian ,
So lightly said.
So heavy a crown
So giant a responsibility.

Chapter 7

Christ like,
Father forgive me for ever proclaiming
Myself Christ-like unthinkingly
By casually wearing the name Christian.

Surely our life must be aimed
Towards a desire to be Christian,
Desire to be Christ-like.
I think only a rare few qualify

In proclaiming themselves a Christian.
I ask you to see me that way
As Abraham the Christian,
The follower of Christ

Then all of my words my actions
Must reflect Christ.
I can do no less and claim that mantle
The honored title Christian, mirror of Christ.

Hold me accountable,
Demand from me
More than I can give,
For our Lord deserves nothing less.

Only with God's strength
Only with my eyes forever on God
Can I even attempt to shoulder this mantle
Abraham Graham, Christian

Your friend in rural Texas

Abraham

*PS please let me know soon regarding your health
Until then I will ask the Lord for His will for you.
A. Graham*

Hannah came back from her Mrs Tilmans
visit bubbly and full of new recipes and crochet patterns
They had been buying yarn at the mercantile

Hannah told Abraham she had a question sent by
Mrs Tilman
Hannah said Mrs Tilman had asked where
Abraham, Hannah and Isaac attended church

Mrs Tilman had explained
That since the Rayner Methodist Church
had closed
The nearest was too far away for her and Mr
Tilman to attend

Mrs Tilman had then asked what Hannah Isaac and
Abraham did for Church
Hannah told her of Abraham talking about his
thoughts about God, their reading scripture
together and singing
Two hymns.

Chapter 7

Mrs Tilman's question was
"Would Abraham mind if she joined them one
Sunday for their family service .
Obviously there was only one answer.

Abraham told Hanna to tell Mrs Tilman she would
be more than welcome
10:00 any Sunday she choose
Hannah was excited
Abraham thoughtful.

Abraham had asked Mr Tilman
About a calf to raise as a milk Cow,
But based on Ruthie's milk out put
He changed his query to one for a mature milk cow.
When delivering Hannah for her Wednesday, visit

Mr Tilman told him
The Everett's on the far side of Rayner
We're having an auction
This coming Saturday.

Mr Tilman and one of his sons were going
because of some calves he had heard of,
He had heard mention of a couple of milk cows
along with chickens goats pigs in the auction.

Abraham thanked him
And when they picked up Hannah
They all agreed to go.
The snow was gone,

And still chilly.
Isaac had started collecting
Boards for a tree house,
After reading the book Swiss Family Robinson.

Hannah was busy crocheting and
Cooking
Abraham puttered about
And prepared for the Saturday morning
Auction trip.

Friday Night Hannah prepared their lunch basket
The auction started at 8:00
Abraham wanted to be there by 7:00
So to be prudent they would leave by 6:00.

A fun day!
Lots of folks
It was not a forced sale
The Everetts were moving to East Texas
to be near their daughter and grandchildren.

Abraham was always surprised at folks
That could leave a life time home
And just move away,
Just pull up roots.

The prices were fair
Mostly,
The milk cows auctioned separately
The first was very expensive,

Chapter 7

The second almost reached as high
But the second bidder dropped out.

They won the bid.
The cow they bought had the name Ernestine
On a tag around her neck.
She came a little high
But it was an auction after all.

Hannah saw some chickens
She wanted and Abraham helped her bid.
She was timid but bid well
And it was $3.00 well spent.

He paid the Auctioneer's wife
For Ernestine and the chickens.
Looked for a way to get Ernestine home
Without having to borrow a trailer.

God provided
For Ernestine was being delivered by
Mr Tilma,
He had room in his trailer.

Three hens and a dozen baby chicks,
Rode complaining, wooden crated in the truck bed.
The children full from lunch
Didn't take too long to nod off on the truck seat.

When they arrived home, Mr Tillman
Had already tied Ernestine to the front porch rail.

She stood patiently waiting.
Isaac, still a little sleepy, untied her and headed
for the barn.

Ruthie was thrilled with Ernestine.
Started acting ten years younger,
They immediately started visiting
Over the stall divider.
Jeroboam was aloof
Looking down on everyone
He pretended not to care,
But his ears gave him away.

Othello herded the new hens
And chicks into the house
Only to be chased out by three mad hens
He strutted around the pen nursing his
wounded pride.

Evening came with a full moon on the horizon.
Hannah cooked ham steaks
Beans that Abraham put back last summer and
A freshly baked loaf of bread with butter.

Saturday night baths over
they gathered round the radio
There was more head nodding
And neck jerking than listening.

Tuckered Abraham called it
So they all headed for their beds

Chapter 7

Hannah was excited,
That Mrs Tilman would be coming
Tomorrow morning.

Chapter 8

Morning
Breakfast and chores done,
Eggs gathered
Barn family fed.

The sun did its best
To pierce the gray,
Sending rays between clouds
As though the sun was preparing an escape,

Maybe to rush spring.
Promising the coming regrowth,
Life colored green
Trees leafed in splendor.

They had cleaned the kitchen,
Swept and dusted the parlor,
Gotten dressed for worship
And at 9:45 there was a knock at the door.
Hannah ran to open it

Welcoming Mrs Tilman in.
Hannah offered her Betsy's old rocker
Brought her a cup of tea
And a napkin.

They all stood
And they bowed the heads in silence
Then Abraham began
"Our Heavenly Father here are four today
Gathered in Your Name,

We are here today to praise You
Here today to thank You,
And most important of all
Here today to learn how to serve You more.

So Lord thank you for Mrs Tilman,
A fine Christian woman, wife, mother,
friend to others, and a grand friend for
our Hannah.

Lord thank you for Hannah, a child of spiritual
beauty as well as physical beauty. Our fine friend
and shining example of love for You,
and our cook whose skills grow better day by day.

And Issac Lord such a fine young man,
Thank you Lord for such an honest hard worker
with a handsome smile,
And wonderful laughter.

Chapter 8

We are here to praise You
and to offer strength to each other in Your Name.

Amen"

It was Hannah's turn to pick the scripture
She picked Psalms 121
And read it to them.

They discussed it,
Mrs Tilman spoke of how she had read
psalm 121 often
When she was worried or during trying times.

Issac requested "Jesus Loves me"
And they finished with one of Abraham's favorites
"Love Lifted Me".

Mrs Tilman rose to go
And told the three in her leaving,
How much she had enjoyed their prayer service.

A fine Sunday evening ended
As Abraham carried. sleeping Issac to bed
And tucked him in.

Othello called roll early,
Crowed up the sun.
Breakfast finished
They loaded up for their trip.

Soon they were in Aspermont,
Dry goods loaded in their truck.
Abraham decided to treat them to a cafe lunch.
The meals were appreciated bu,
The deserts were loved!

Hannah had cake and Issac had a large piece
of apple pie
with a slice of melted cheese on top.
The marshal came in and joined them for coffee.

Abraham thanked him for telling his sister.
The Marshall said his brother-in-law had thanked
him already
for telling him of the farm.

With HJ's latest letter
tucked securely in his overall bib,
And cafe full stomachs,
They headed home.

Issac's job now,
overseen by Abraham
Was to milk Ernestine.
No small task because of her large quantity of milk.

With more hens Hannah was gathering eggs three
times a day
She had made arrangements this
Last visit
To sell extra eggs for 1 cent per egg

Chapter 8

To the mercantile.
The money would belong to her.

She was excited
Tonight's supper was different
A tinned stew, canned vegetables
Fresh bread, fresh butter and Hannah's first cobbler from canned peaches.

A radio show
Quickly giving way to drooping eyes.
Prayers of thanksgiving then
Early to bed after a really full day.

Abraham made a cup of Postum
Sat at the table
And begin to read.

My Dear Abraham

My balance seems to be diminishing, and I have fallen,
A few times. The Lord has seen fit to cushion my falls
So nothing has broken, however my travels have become
More limited. Fear not my dear friend, all is well.

I have upon reading your last letter, been
re-evaluating my
Use of the word Christian.
It is amazing how we throw this word around
thoughtlessly.

*The cost Christ paid for our forgiveness treated casually is
indefensible!*

*Understanding complete and selfless forgiveness,
may be beyond the human grasp.
I believe the Great Jehovah sees us through His son
Jesus Christ,
thus we appear sin free.*

*I am afraid I must offend my Lord.
My guilt, and self recrimination
must cause him pain.
For it must appear to God to negate the sacrifice of
His only son.*

*Aah but it must please the devil
For we lowly beings to carry guilt for forgiven sins.
Would not satan strut with pride
Boasting of this accomplishment.*

*I understand the posture of the sinner,
The burden of guilt for past sins and failures,
I know not the bearing of a forgiven man
A redeemed soul.*

*So much to discuss
With my brethren
Oh if you could only be there in person
We will indeed however, relish your letter*

Chapter 8

Yours in Christ

HJ

Abraham had never asked HJ's age
But, based on this letter he must be older than
Abraham had assumed
Going to the parlor he took HJ's book from
the book case
And read "The Author" from the back cover

Based on information gleaned from
His book HJ would be 93 years of age
Abraham was surprised
Thinking him a much younger man

After turning in that Monday night,
His thoughts and prayers were all for his friend HJ
And of course for the children.
No concerns, just thanking and praising the Lord
For his time with them.

The days flew by
The following Sunday,
Mrs Tilman came again,
She had a fine voice.

The next Wednesday,
Experiencing seemingly spring like weather,
A strange car came up their road
And pulled up at their gate.

They watched from the front porch
As the Marshal from Aspermont
Dismounted and walked up to their house
Abraham welcomed him warmly.
And offered him a chair
They talked for some minutes
Weather and pleasantries
Then the Marshal whom Abraham now called Newt
Asked if he could speak with Abraham privately.

Sending the children to do their chores
He promised them that the Marshal
would not leave
without saying goodbye.
Visitors were rare, and a cause for excitement.

Newt told him
The Sheriff of Stonewall Country,
A personal friend, had received a bulletin
from Plains Texas.

The body of a man was recovered
From a car caught in a flash flood
Last November.
During the investigation,
In amongst his meager belongings,
Was his name Winston Roland Albright.

A flyer advertising jobs in California,
A water soaked Bible with his name were found.

Chapter 8

The Bible also listed his wife's name Ella
Mae Albright
With a line drawn through it and the word dead
written over it.

Then two children Hannah Marie Albright and
Issac Paul Albright
With no children's bodies found.
A bulletin was sent out to local counties.

Mail and large amounts of bulletins
Had prevented this
from coming to light
until recently.

Abraham was quiet
Sadden by the news
One it would be hard to tell the children,
And two he was concerned over the disposition of
the children
Now that it was in the hands of the law.

Ned said "I'd not worry. I will tell the sheriff the
children were abandoned
By a road outside of Aspermont
And taken in by a good family
They are now safe and well looked after.

I think the country will be relieved not to have to
house or place them.

I will let you know the outcome when I
see you next"
Abraham thanked him over and over
For his trip and time

The children arrived in time to say good bye
And waved as he drove off.
Abraham asked Hannah to fix three cups of coco
and bring them to the parlor
He then sent Issac to wash off.

Evidently in Issac's hurry to see Ned again
He had neglected part of his washing up,
At least the backs of his hands
And his neck.

All three, armed with their cups of coco
Sat in the parlor as Abraham
Explained the reason for Ned's visit.
Abraham tried to be honest

But he hoped God would forgive
him if he left the impression
Mr Albright had been on his way back,
To pick up the children.

For indeed no one knew
which way the car had been traveling
when hit by the flood.

Chapter 8

Complete silence,
No tears
Perhaps a sniffle from Issac.
Issac then whispered in Hannah's ear
And she said in a small voice.

"Does this mean the Sheriff will take us away?"
Abraham said the Marshall doesn't think that
will happen,
But what we must remember above all
Is in whose hands must we place all of this.

The three figures slide to the floor
and kneeling
prayed quietly.

The week wore on slowly
Hannah came in the next Wednesday
to announce on her way home from Mrs. Tilman
She had seen several trees budding.
She said she hoped that they would still be here in
the spring

Reminding Abraham
He was not the only one in pain.
He gathered the three in the parlor
After supper and they kneeled once again praying

Issac,
head bowed,
Said "Dear God

Please don't make us leave,

I like it here, I know you love us ,
so please let us stay forever.
Thank you
This is Issac"

Hannah next, head bowed
"Lord Jesus
This gift you have given Issac and I is special.
This person has blessed our lives,
And taught so much about your love and mercy.

Issac and I will go where you send us
We will go Joyfully,
But I hope you let us stay here Lord
We love Abraham so much
Thank you Lord
Amen"

Abraham choked and waited til
He could speak clearly
Then he spoke.

"Our Dear Heavenly Father
These children have said it all
I love them so, I have been so blessed by
their presence
We three wait on you Lord
All in Your time Lord
Amen"

Chapter 8

The days crawled by
until the Sunday before their Aspermont trip

Services ready,
At 9:45 Mrs Tilman once again knocked on the door
Then asked "is it alright I brought a guest?"

Mr Tilman in his overalls and a suit coat
followed her into the parlor
The small group prayed, sang, then Abraham
talked about the Bible.

And they ended with a prayer
from Mr Tilman

Hannah Issac and Abraham agreed
it was a good prayer time and nice the
Tilmans came.
Sunday dinner was great
Hannah's cooking was growing by the day.

The night before the next Aspermont trip
Abraham sat at the table
And wrote to his friend.

My Dear HJ

I am sorry to hear of your falling
But so thankful to hear of the Lord's cushioning.
As we have said many times
He is "ever Faithful."

The mantel of guilt is so familiar,
Claiming a sinless life does indeed go against a sinner's nature.
I believe we find a dark comfort in our guilt and shame.
Satan knows his craft well.

I would never boast,
When speaking of being redeemed.
No works can earn this gift of a sinless self
For it was paid for by the blood of our Christ.

As in so many of our letters
Self once again rears its ugly head,
Peering from behind the Cross.

For is it not just as egotistical
To claim the position of worst,
as it is to claim the position of better.

Self has nothing to do with our salvation.
The Lord's mercy being our only bragging point
We may boast only of the kindness of our loving God.

A possible challenge has arisen
The children's father's body was found.
Having died as the results of a west Texas flash flood.

The care of the children
May be taken over by the county.
Of course this may be my fear speaking.

Chapter 8

It is far too early to know
What the counties disposition of the children will be,
And I must continually remind my self
They belong to the Lord.

To think anything else would be foolhardy indeed.
I do admit to occasional fear,
But once given to the Lord
I am free.

I am blessed to have this time
Between now and learning of the disposition
To love, cherish,
And speak of our Lord to these two beautiful souls.

My time
to fortify
To reinforce
To prepare them
were they to be placed elsewhere.
So they will be well equipped spiritually.

A new journey for me,
Accepting God's plan.
Though the self is in pain
I will try Joyfully to accept His will.

I praise the Lord for His Wisdom,
And I am thankful for every moment
These children are and have been shared with me
God is truly great.

*"Not my will oh Lord but thine be done
Amen"*

Your friend Abraham

Morning came early,
Othello crowed proud and loud,
Chores done,
They soon damped down the fires
And climbed into the pickup truck.

Everyone was quiet on the trip to town
The truck tossed them about
The air was chilly but not bitter cold
A few early wildflowers waved from the side
of the road.

Arriving in Aspermont Abraham and the
children both
Watched for Newt,
While shopping, mailing his letter
Then siting out front of the Mercantile.

Abraham again treated them to the cafe
This time just stalling for extra time to see Newt.
They ate well but all three watched the door.
He didn't come

Chapter 9

Nature knew,
Othello knew.
The barn family knew.
It was Spring!

On the way back from the outhouse
Trees budding,
Promise
No longer maybe.

God's promise
Today,
Abraham knew!
God was leaving the children here.

A feeling,
A knowing,
A new peace,
A reassurance.

Hannah was forking over the bacon
Issac was putting out the silverware.
Abraham poured a cup of coffee for himself,

And two coffee milks with lots of sugar.

They held hands round the old kitchen table
And Abraham said,
"Thank you Lord!
For this life,
For this home,
For the blessings, far to numerous to number.

For these beautiful young souls
Listening and learning of you,
And my joy in watching them grow.

For these eggs from Hannah's chickens,
For this bacon from Issac's pigs,
For our breath oh Lord Amen."

"AND" said Hannah quickly,
"Lord for Abraham Graham
Who picked Issac and I from the side of the road.
Loved us as his own cherished children,

Teaching us of you.
But most of all Lord
Showed us in his daily life, Lord,
How to live for you,
Amen."

Abraham eyes brimming over,
Coughed into his bandana,
And busied himself buttering a fluffy big biscuit

Chapter 9

To sop up some egg yolk.

It was a Friday morning,
Hannah asked
"When do we plant our garden?
What seeds do we need?"

Abraham say "Monday would be a good
planting day.
We can move those seedlings
The ones we started in the feed room of the barn,
I think we have had the last frost"

"Tell me about the little orchard, she said
Just past the Garden.
Every tree has buds
What type of trees are they?"
Asked Hannah.

Abraham looked at Hannah,
With new eyes,
Long thick dark blond to brown hair,
White blue eyes,
Guess some would say startling.
Long eye lashes,
A captivating smile,
What an amazing task
God had assigned Abraham.

This child woman,
A fertile soul

To plant the seeds of God,
Love and Awe for the Grand Creator.

An open heart listening for God's voice,
A willingness to follow without question,
A heart to praise and offer thanks,
The knowledge to place God above all in her life.

"Abraham Abraham!
"What kind of trees are those?"
Hannah repeated,
Abraham laughed,
"Sorry honey, he smiled, guess I was wool gathering,
2 Apple, 2 peach, 2 pear and 2 figs."

"Not much fruit the last few years,
But who knows"
Abraham picked up his plate almost wiped clean
With his "sopping" biscuit
In pursuit of the last of the yolk,

Slid it into the soapy water in the dish basin.
Took the large bar of lye soap,
Soaped the dish rag,
And washed the dinners plates
As Issac pushed up beside him

Ready to dry.
Issac adjusted his stance to stand like Abraham,
And said in voice trying to sound like Abraham,
"Bring'm on, can't dry'um, if you ain't washing."

Chapter 9

Such a full heart.
Thank you Lord, Thank you Lord
Guide me Lord,
Let me follow your plan for these two.

Sunday's were always five now
And they had started swapping houses.
This Sunday it was the Tilman's house
and there were rumors of a new couple coming.

The Thomas's,
Lived about a mile or so past Mr and Mrs Tilman.
Abraham thought he'd met Mr Thomas a
few years ago
But he wasn't sure.

All dressed up
Bibles in hand,
Hannah and Issac Albright
And Abraham Graham

Drove into the Tilman's gate
To see two
Different trucks,
They met everyone inside.

Eight people met Sunday
To praise and worship our Lord.
The Thomas's and the widow Wilson,
Jeroboam's former owner.

Hymns well sung,
a might louder
And with gusto,
A prayer by Mr Thomas.

Then Mr Tilman asked
if Abraham would speak.
There was no question
For Abraham could not refuse.

"I was thinking on the way here
Could a man be more blessed
Than I.
Today I meet with old and new friends
To talk of our Lord.

To share stories of His blessings,
To offer support in times of trials,
It is such an honor to speak of a God,
Who loved old this Abraham Graham so much,

That He allowed His only son Jesus
To hang from a cross and die,
Just to free me from my sins.

Me! You!
It is beyond my understanding,
It is to great for me to conceive of,
So I can only say thank you Lord.

I would also like to sing my favorite

Chapter 9

Hymn
"Oh How I Love Jesus."

They visited over coffee supplied by the Tilmans.
Mr Thomas was a quiet man strong and
appearing gentle,
Very pretty, talkative wife.

Hannah and Issac cornered Widow Wilson,
Swapping Jeroboam's tales and laughing.
Widow Wilson was so happy to know of his health
and how much the children loved and spoiled him.

Monday morning came quickly.
An unscheduled trip to Aspermont
Pretending to need nails for Issac's treehouse,
Crochet and baking supplies for Hannah.

After only a few minutes in the mercantile,
The Marshall came through the door
And greeted everyone.
Newt apologized for missing them
On their last trip.

Seems there had been a cattle rustling,
And an argument started in town.
A shooting,
A man was wounded,
And Newt was needed.

He said he hadn't heard anything,

But he would use his office telephone
To contact the Plains town Sheriff
If they could wait.
Since it was on a bulletin
he could say it was official business.

He left for his office and Abraham went to the post office.
A letter from HJ,
And a letter from the bank saying
$6,100 had been deposited in an account for Abraham Graham.

They sat in the cafe for what seemed like forever,
Then in front of the mercantile.
Finally they spied the Marshal
Crossing the street.

He told Abraham
The Plains town Marshall
Had handed the information
To the county judge

And had assumed it settled.
Newt then said he called the courthouse.
The county clerk said the Judge
Had closed the case
Since the children were safely housed.

The county clerk would send a letter of disposition, and some papers

Chapter 9

For Abraham,
care of Aspermont General delivery.
Abraham just sat,
Thanked Newt profusely,
Loaded up his family
And headed home.

Abraham said to Hannah and Issac
It's done,
You are to stay with me
Until you decide to leave.

The children screamed
bounced around in the seat
Thanking and praising God.

Abraham had to stop the truck
because the hugs were interfering
With his driving.
Of course he didn't care
After all who would not prefer hugs to driving?

Home for supper,
Ham steaks,
Canned vegetables,
Pie.

Cleanup done,
Kids in the parlor,
Radio on,
Abraham opened his letter.

Abraham
My brother!

We are in prayer!

I have contacted the group to a man.
We are praying for you and the children's peace.
For joy in accepting God's will.
It is indeed a challenge
To find joy in accepting God's will,
Especially when it runs contrary to ours.
We know intellectually God's way is the only right way.

But our "self" knows so strongly
What it wants,
The battle can be fierce
And bloody.

You are also so right!
This isn't about you,
It is truly God's will for these to souls
That matters.
I know without question
How blessed they have been to be with you.

If the Lord chooses to move them
It will be best for them and for you.
Though my limited human sight
And self, could not imagine a better place
This side of heaven.

Chapter 9

I am going to thank God for His wisdom
In knowing the best place for Hannah and Issac.
I am going to also thank God for His wisdom
In knowing what's best for you.

Though I still will tell Him my meager opinion,
He knows and smiles when I do.
I believe firmly in my heart
Hannah and Issac are home.

Yours in constant Prayer
HJ

Thank you Lord
For these men that pray.
Lord take from me the reins
These children are yours.
Please help me remember this
Help me never think of them as mine.
They are solely your charges,
Guide me.

Though sleep was slow in coming
Abraham finally slept deeply,
And only Othello's persistence
Caused Abraham to wake.

It was obvious.
A sparkle to the day,
Issac appeared jubilant,
As he searched for a tree

For his tree house.

Early afternoon,
The three brought the seedlings
From the barn
And started their spring garden.

Seeds tomorrow,
A visit to Mrs Tilman for Hannah
To share the news and
Finish her lasted crocheted throw.

Before bed Abraham sat at the table
Licked his pencil point
And began.

HJ and Friends

Your prayers and mine were answered
Though I have not received a paper
The sheriff and the county clerk of Yoakum County
Have confirmed there will be no further action needed
For the children
Now that they are safely housed and cared for.

We have celebrated .
I'm sure the Lord is deafened
By our thanks and praise,
And I realize the responsibilities are even greater .

I was looking through the hymns

Chapter 9

and I ran across "Sweet Hour of Prayer".
A beautiful hymn,
I wondered if I could pray
An hour.

I started by remembering that day
The bundle on the side of the road.
What if I hadn't noticed
What if someone had come before me,

I thanked the Lord profusely.
Thinking of their gentle and malleable nature their curiosity.
They learn of the Lord with joy
I find I am distracted by the children.

I am no longer praying!
In less than a minute of my hour prayer.
I return to prayer only to become
Distracted once more.

Now I understand the apostles
In Gethsemane,
Though I would act as Christ if I could,
I find I mirror the common man.

I would behave only as Christ
But I follow in Thomas's
Peter's and Paul's footsteps,
Though never equaling their stature.

My thought is this.
"Is my Christ like behavior
Due only to these two children,
Or is it due all,
in my life?
Should I not in my behavior
Seek to impart The Lord
to the clerk in the mercantile,
To the waitress in the cafe?

Not just a smile
But also allow a glimpse of God
In my behavior,
Remind a stranger of God.

Not just in words,
For that is easy,
And oft times
Misconstrued.

My entire behavior,
Bearing,
Thoughtfulness ,
I do so desire to mirror my Lord.

Thank everyone for their prayers
For our small family.

Your faithful friend
Abraham

Chapter 9

Folding the letter
he slid it into the envelope
Licked the flap,
and addressed it.

Placing it in his denim jumper pocket
Abraham undressed for bed,
Sleeping in his Union suit
As was his custom.

He stared into his face
in his wardrobe mirror by his bed
Does anyone see God
In this face?
So heavily wrinkled,
Weather worn,
Smile cracked,
Yet still familiar?

God Loves you Abraham Graham,
God trusts you to raise
Two beautiful souls,
To know and trust the Lord
Implicitly.

What a task!
Joyous
Yet serious,
A life task.

The bed springs song this night was short,
Abraham was exhausted .
He slept hard
And was slow to rise.

He found Hannah cooking breakfast already,
It might be just him
But she seemed happier more at home
Than before.

There was a small moment
When she appeared grown.
Bringing a quick sadness
At the thought of the two growing up.

Soon forgotten as Issac
Sleepy headed appeared in his place.
Puffy eyes, hair going every-which way,
Putting his glass back on the table
He gave a milk surrounded sheepish smile.

Such a beautiful budding man of God,
Oh my sweet Betsy
If you were only here,
You would have loved this so much.
And what a shining example you would have been!

Chapter 10

So unexpected,
A new mule,
A new milk cow,
Pig family growing.

Three times as many chickens,
Garden plot almost doubled,
Fence being mended
For a possible calf or two.

A coming busy time of the year
Spring,
Growth
Green.

Last April it was just
Abraham,
Old aged
Winding down.

This year
Promise,
So much to teach

To explain.

The garden enlarged for three,
The orchard renewing,
Canning,
Abraham's 79th Birthday

Soon it will be loft weather,
That made Abraham smile,
Though he was sure this year
His time there would be shorter and louder.

Cabbage, beans, peas, corn,
Beets, potatoes, okra
Planting weeding harvest canning
A major time for learning.

The orchard was different
Too late to prune,
Just have to make do this year
Prune in the fall for next year.

Something has changed
Abraham took off his hat and wiped his
rugged old face
With is old bandana.
The sun was a might warm today

His books of late had not called him.
The theologians, philosophers, great thinkers
were mute.

Chapter 10

God had been speaking through Hanna and Issac
A simple fact, a simple faith.

Abraham had a new confidant,
A new listener,
A voiceless provocateur,
A poser of questions unanswerable .

What if,
Why,
When,
Are you sure?

Jeroboam.
His garden companion,
His "long-eared" professor
Puller of the plow.

Strange relationship this,
In all honesty
Abraham was more familiar
With jeroboam's rear than face.

Boney
No matter the feed.
Age was robbing Jeroboam
Of muscle and mass.

Following behind
A mule butt,
Watching Jeroboam's ears

They talked of the Lord.

Stands to reason
Jeroboam was innocent.
He knew no sin,
No malice,

No soul?
Maybe,
Gods child?
Probably not,

Gods creation?
Absolutely!
Loved by God
Without a doubt.

Are not two sparrows sold for a farthing?
and one of them shall not fall on the ground
without your Father.
Mathew 10:29

So this Thursday Morning
Hannah made breakfast
And Issac was working in the orchard.
Abraham said out loud,

"So tell me Jeroboam
You've lived a lot of years
Even for a mule,
Do you believe in God?"

Chapter 10

Lots of ear twitching,
Listening to Abraham's voice,
They stopped at the end of the row.

He laid the plow over
And walked to Jeroboam's head.
Rubbed his long ears
Smelling that mule smell,

A nice aroma,
A familiar oder,
Down to earth
Safe smell.

Totally white faced now,
Deep brown eyes,
Lips twitching ,
hoping for a carrot.

He looked into Jeroboam's face
Again
And repeated ,
"Do you believe in God?"

The answer in Abraham's head
Was instant.
"Of course
How could you not?"

"Might as well ask
Do I believe in air,

I breathe therefore
I believe."

Abraham thought
As Jeroboam spoke,
If animals accept God without doubt
Then what's to doubt?

You do what you do,
If it was right you can do it again,
If wrong,
Don't do it again.

Is it's man's lot?
Wining free choice
Means man can doubt God,
Therefore he can doubt himself.

Free choice
Leaves us free to doubt,
To question,
Come to believe by our own intent.

Issac's evening prayers
Were simple
To the point
Innocent .

"Lord, we're in the kitchen
Hannah's a real good cook
Abraham takes good care of us

Chapter 10

Help me a good boy,

Thank you for a fine supper"
Amen

Abraham's prayers more complex
Asking for guidance,
For understanding
For help.

Why not,

"Lord I'm in the garden,
Hannah and Issac
Are healthy and happy,
You take excellent care of us,

Help us be better Christians.
Thank you for today,
Amen
The back screen door bangs
And here comes Hannah.
A half a bacon and tomatoes sandwich,
And a jar of fresh well water.

The Sunday service still growing
Has reached 15 people.
Everyone's living room is too small,
Soon time to make a decision.

A town trip for supplies

and a couple of letters, one from Fort Worth,
one from County Clerk Yoakum County Texas.

My dear Abraham

We are thrilled
Though none surprised.
Your conscientious acceptance
And guardian of the two children

Is exemplary,
A wise approach to
Bring up children
In the Christian life.

So much of young parents time
Is spent in surviving
Making a living
Personal learning.

It is amazing
We have time to teach the children anything.
That's where the grandparents
Are valuable.

You have taken over both roles,
And God knew you could
And would,
Indeed a blessing.
As for singing
"Sweet Hour of Prayer",

Chapter 10

It is a favorite hymn
Of our entire little group.

But alas also a reminder
Of our weakness,
Our Achilles heel,
For everyone of us had a different
Idea of prayer.

Praying for an hour
We tried,
To a man,
A seemingly simple task
But with no success.

The general consensus of opinion being,

It takes at least an hour and a half
To pray for an hour,
But a majority of us fall asleep.

So we, thinking ourselves wise,
Give way to wandering thoughts
short attention spans
And sleep.

Perhaps we take the freedom to pray
Anytime we want to
Too casually,
To much for granted.

I am thankful
For My Lord
And for the fact He hears
And answers.

My friend
I know you know
The Lord has truly blessed
You three.

Your friend HJ

Abraham thought of his conversations
With Jeroboam.
Do animals pray
What do they pray for,

Is prayer for request only?
Praise,
Questions,
What is prayer?

Opening the letter from the county Clerk,
He read with praise and thanks.

To Mr Abraham
Rayner, Texas

In accordance with the Sheriff of Plains
Texas's report

Chapter 10

on the accidental death of Winston
Rolland Albright,
Widower of Ella Mae Albright, father to Hannah
and Issac Albright.

The children will be left in the care of
Mr Abraham Graham.Rayner Texas
To be cared for and raised in a healthy safe manner.
Enclosed find a form for Texas state adoption.

Adoption is not required for guardianship,
But is available upon filling out the required form
in front of a county judge.

Address any questions to
Horace C. Wright
Yoakum County Clerk
Yoakum County Court House
Plain Texas.

Adoption,
Never thought of it.
Seemed that should be
Hannah and Issac's decision.

Abraham decided
To give the letter to Hannah
and let them talk it over and decide.
They could let him know.

The next morning after breakfast

Abraham gave the letter to Hannah telling her.
"This is a matter for you and Issac to consider"
Lots of private conversations,
And during the rest of the day.

Supper was unusually quiet.
After everything was cleared away
And before Bible reading,
Hannah and Issac came and stood in front
of Abraham.

Hannah said
"Abraham if you adopted Issac and me,
Would that mean we would be Hannah and
Issac Graham?"
Abraham nodded solemnly.

"Would that mean we could call you father?"
Again Abraham nodded.

"Forever?"
And Abraham nodded once again.

Then
Hannah and Issac took each other's hand and
Hannah said
"Then will you please adopt us".

Abraham held open his arms
and said "it would give me great pleasure
to adopt you two beautiful children"

Chapter 10

Lots of hugging and kissing
Before bed.

Late night at the kitchen table, Abraham wrote,

HJ

I've been thinking.
Betsy always said I pondered on stuff to much.

The subject of prayer.

So many of us
Use prayer as a want list,
A "please God fix it" list.
My fear is what if I don't know what's best,

What if only God knows.
What if I say "please God let my wife live"
And she suffers in pain and misery
for many more years.

So my only prayer should be one of thanksgiving.
"Thank you Lord, that you knew best,
Thank you Lord, that you are the leader of my life,
Thank you Lord for blessed decisions".

Though I could as a child of God
Pray "Lord, I am afraid of life without my wife,
I am afraid of the loneliness

Afraid of my sorrow".

*I guess the true answer is
Whether for one minute
Or one hour,
Be honest with the Lord.*

*He understands us
As his children.
You can say
"Lord I know what you decide for me is best,
I know I'll be happier with what you have chosen for me
than anything I can think of.*

*Faith, again, of a child
I am trying to turn my prayers
To thank you's.
How do you thank God
For the ultimate sacrifice?*

*How do you ask something
Of someone who's given you
more than you deserve?*

*Only the Lord Jehovah
The great "I Am"
Can be asked for a good crop,
After sacrificing His only Son.*

*We are indeed
God's needy Children.*

Chapter 10

Your Friend in Christ
Abraham

Morning and paper work,
Breakfast done
Clean up over,
Hannah wanted to fill out the adoption form
right away.

So Issac and Abraham sat and watched
As Hannah took over.
Reading asking questions
And occasionally
Licking the point of her pencil.

He heard father five times before breakfast was over.
"Betsy are you listening
I do wish you were here",
Who knew that word father could feel like that.

Abraham had to talk Hannah
out of making a special trip to town
Just to mail the adoption form.

But a small working farm demanded chores
Be done,
Then there was school work
And animals to care for.

Several men of the Sunday group
Are getting together
To look at the old Rayner Methodist
Church building.
The meeting is growing
And most folks houses aren't big enough.

The building is available
For $120 with an acre of land.
If the building is repairable
The group have agreed to purchase it,
And start meeting there on Sundays.

It's a long drive but even Newt,
The marshal from Aspermont and is wife Cindy
Have come to a Sunday meeting twice.
Seems these Sunday mornings are spirit filled.

Abraham felt the need to listen
To think, to talk to God
So he harnessed up Jeroboam.

The Garden was plowed but
They plowed anyway.
Abraham picked a soft ground area
And they leisurely walked the ground.

It wasn't to late,
They might plant a few watermelons
What do you think Jeroboam?
But today Jeroboam kept his own counsel.

Chapter 10

Abraham wondered
What does God do
When Hannah, Issac and Abraham Graham's
Lives appear to be going smoothly.

I guess that would be the prayer
"Heavenly Father
We know the perils of this world
Hidden dangers, thorns and tares,

Thank you for going before us
For making our way safe,
Forgive us for our child-like complacency"

Jeroboam turned his head back
To see why Abraham had paused,
They turned and finished the third row
"Lord thank you".

It was that night Abraham
Was taught a lesson
By Hannah and Issac.

Hannah's evening prayer

"Dear God
Thank you for our lives,
Thank you for Abraham,
Issac and I loved our mother
And father,
We don't mean to disrespect them

By asking Abraham to adopt us.

We needed someone to teach us,
To love us to guide us,
To protect us,
You gave us Abraham.
We think that was wise.

Will you tell our mother and father
We are fine and we love them.
Thank you
From Hannah and Issac
Amen"

Chapter 11

Abraham heard the wail,
All the way out by the well
And went running for the barn
Hannah beat him.

Issac's arm was not supposed to bend there.
An attempt to swing out of the hayloft failed,
A meeting with the ground
Broke Issac's arm.

Tears, lots of sister attention,
A slow but still painful ride,
And they arrived in Aspermont.

The Doctor,
 Some more tears,
A splint and sling,
Then to the mercantile for licorice whips.

The cafe supplied an over due lunch,
And some laughter at Issac
Eating with his left hand.
A bonus nice visit with Newt.

No letter from HJ,
And a seed was sown
Worry,
What if?

Abraham never shook his hand,
Heard his voice.
This man of God
Mountain of faith.

Abraham left the kids with
Newt,
And went over to the railway station
Just for information
That's all.

One adult, two children
Round trip to Fort Worth
$28.
Changing trains
About 14 hours each way.

With things going well on the farm
Totally do-able.
If HJ was still healthy,
Course it would have to wait until
Issac's arm was healed.

A not too painful ride home for Issac,
And Hannah made a small supper.
Fresh milk, egg and bacon sandwiches

On fresh baked bread.
Soon everyone was ready for bed.

Abraham a little too worried
Decided to write a quick letter to HJ.
A coal oil lamp lit
And a half used pencil,
He licked the point and started.

My Dear Friend HJ

No word from you,
Pardon my concern.
We of latter years
Are more tenuous .

Often giving way to worries about health
And longevity.
I had to write
We are well, are you?

These letters have become
An important part of my Life.
I need an adult to hear of my Lord
To teach me, give me new insight.

True I have Jeroboam,
Indeed the children talk of God,
But you, my teacher my questioner
Spark my fires, initiate my journeys.

There is so much more of the Lord
I would know,
New revelations,
Bring comfort and a new closeness.

Gods little ones here
Continue to grow,
But some lessons are more painful
Than others.

Issac broke his arm today
Making it necessary to take a trip to town.
I stopped by the railroad station
And priced tickets to Fort Worth.

It is within our means
If you or someone you know
could suggest a reasonable hotel,
We would like to visit you.

From a widower in a hayloft
Unfettered,
To a surrogate father
And friend to an amazing Christian author,
I now have ties to my heart.

It will be after the first of August
Issac's arm should be healed.
The first and perhaps second harvest of the garden
canned.
Please let us know.

Chapter 11

I have revised my praying
To praise and thankfulness.
I am surprised at the peace it affords.
No am no longer frantic for solutions.

I now thank the Lord for the outcome.
It worries me, it seems so easy.
I have thanked the Lord profusely
For your friendship.

I pray a visit would not burden you
Or inconvenience you
In any way.

Hoping to meet you in the flesh in August

Abraham

Deep restful sleep, Othello,
And the smell of Hannah's breakfast.
An amazing young lady
A brilliant student.

She would soon reach the stage
Where a decision about a higher education
Would be necessary.
A troubling thought.

They just came into his life!
Letting go would be hard.
Remembering they were the Lords

Would bring the peace Abraham would need.

After breakfast the three discussed
The trip to Fort Worth.
Hannah and Issac were excited
And couldn't stop talking.

The old Methodist church building
Was purchased.
Renovations were started,
And last Sunday was the first Sunday
In the new building.

24 people.
They asked if Abraham would consider being interim pastor
He told them he would pray about it,
It was more than he wanted.

Mrs Tilman is coming Tuesday
To teach the three of us
How to better can for the winter
Our garden is over-flowing.

We have to pick up the canning jars
We ordered them last trip
When Issac got his arm set.
We are going Monday after next.

I am in earnest prayer
In hopes of a letter.

Chapter 11

I pray I have not waited to long
I'm afraid for my friend.

A beautiful Sunday,
The Church smelled of wildflowers,
And fresh cut lumber and paint.
Brother Tilman spoke of his
Youth and finding the Lord.

Brothers Baskin spoke eloquently
Such an impressive man.
He spoke of his herd
A dairy farmer.

God in his life, and their nine children,
He teared up as he spoke of his blessings.
His wife, front row smiled and wiped her eyes as well,
Such a fine group of Christians.

Monday morning
Aspermont bound.
The summer declared it's reign official,
With brilliant greens and sunlight.

The truck front seat
Graham filled,
Rattled and muttered
It's song of travel.

Bouncing along full of breakfast

An early morning summer rain
Made the heat heavy
So the windows were out.

Hannah and one armed Issac
Loaded jars and supplies
At the mercantile,
as he headed for the Post office.

Two Letters!
One from HJ,
And one from the Yoakum County Magistrate.

Opening the legal document first
He found an adoption form
To be signed by a Local judge or Justice of the peace
To finalize the adoption .

With the two youngsters
Leading the way
The threesome soon found
Aspermont's JP.

Harvey Climpson gave Abraham the look
He reserved for all the men
that cut their own hair,
Harvey was Aspermont's barber and JP.

Hannah and Issac's signatures
Along with Abraham and Harvey Climpson JP,
And Hannah and Issac became Graham's,

Chapter 11

and Abraham finally became a father.

25 cents each
A gift from their "father"
To celebrate their adoption,
And they rushed back into the Mercantile.

Abraham perched on the front bench
Just out of the sun
And checking the date stamp
Read the HJ's letter.

My dear Abraham

Please forgive the tardiness
Of my letter.
An illness started in out little home here
And infected all our residents.

We lost two of our family
Due to pneumonia
But the rest of us are recovering.
The halls echo to the sounds
Of coughing and nose blowing

But we survive.
Summer colds
Seem just has hard as
Their brothers the winter colds.

The Lord offers me a peace

That passes understanding.
During my darker hours
I think of loved ones waiting,

And upon starting recovery
I was cheered by the thought
Of my prayer group,
And my three friends in Rayner.
Days of absence ,
And age both cause my anticipation
To grow.
Watching friends pass on before you
Reminds me of my nearness.

My time of calling,
My moment of rejoicing,
My welcome home,
My promised reward.

Ah but my friend
Strange this feeling
I have developed for you
My mentor, challenger.

Opening my eyes and heart
To a broader understanding of my lord.
I know God has a reason for your
Staying.

The charges He has entrusted to you
Evidence His

Chapter 11

Pride in you
And your faith in Him.

I am recovering and feeling stronger,
Looking forward to our "prayer" meeting.
Such good and loyal friends
If you could only meet them.

Your brother in Christ
HJ

Steam, heat
Tables, chairs,
Covering the floor over in the corner
Jars of canned vegetables

Everywhere.

A bouquet of colored glass
God's generous bounty.
Mrs Tilman, Hannah,
And even one-armed Issac

All preparing food for winter.
Sweat and cool well water helped
It was a momentous project for all.

Abraham's job
Was filling the shelves in the storm cellar.
After a thorough cleaning
By orders of Hanna.

Mrs Tilman would approve a batch,
And Abraham would move them to the cellar.
It appeared they would fill the shelves
They hadn't been filled in years.

After much prayer and contemplation
Abraham informed their Sunday group
He would do his best
to have something to say on Sundays,
Or call on somebody that did.

A trip to town to have the Doctor
Look at Issac's arm,
A few supplies
and another letter from HJ.

The Doctor said Issac healed fast
And he removed the splint,
Requesting that Issac use a sling
For the next seven to ten days.

Hannah and Issac had money
of their own and sat happily
On the truck bed
While Abraham read his letter.

Abraham

I just received your second letter
I'm am so sorry you worried
As I explained in my last letter,

Chapter 11

I was "under the weather.

A VISIT!!
What a joy!
I am excited
I told my prayer group.

They are also excited
Edgar offered his home for your visit
Rather than a hotel.
A wonderful soul.

Edgar was widowed
Several years ago,
After raising a family of seven
And now lives alone in a massive house.

He would be thrilled and honored
If you would accept his invitation.
He so longs to hear children's
Voices once more in his home.

He retired at the the end of this year
From the theology Department
Of Southwestern,
And plans to write and study more
He would love some time with you.

I can hardly contain my joy
at the thought of shaking your hand,
And seeing God's two little ones

In the flesh.

Write soon with your time of arrival
Your thoroughly excited brother in Christ.

HJ

Abraham waved at Issac and Hannah
To go back into the mercantile
A new pair of jeans for Issac,
A new dress for Hannah,

New overalls and Denim shirt for Abraham.
Store bought socks
And a shirt for Issac,

And they were ready for Fort Worth.
There was lots of excitement
On the way home
And plans to finalize.

Abraham wrote a quick note to HJ
Announcing the date,
Contacted Mr Tilman
To watch over the farm,

And time drew near.
They prayed,
Laid out their trip
And asked for God's help and guidance.

Chapter 12

Hannah packed
Some cheese,
Bacon and tomato sandwiches
A few apples from the orchard.
Some left over ham

Hannah and Issac's clothes.
Fit in a carpet bag Betsy once used
When she went to see her folks.
Abraham had an old cardboard
Suitcase seemed it would still hold up.

Everybody fed and packed
They loaded up the truck.
Due to the anticipation
They were ready a little early.

The excitement had already made Issac tired
So he slept in the front seat
Head in Hannah's lap.

Reaching Aspermont
They left the truck

Behind Newt's office,
He had said he would keep an eye on it.

Breakfast in the cafe finished,
Extra biscuits added to Hannahs,
Packed basket and the train platform
waiting to leave,
Abraham pulled his pencil from
His pocket.

He laid a piece of paper on his suitcase
Perched on his knees,,
Licked his pencil point and began

My Dear HJ

We are on the way!
Sitting on the depot platform
But I still need to write a letter.
When the thoughts and words boil over

I would not lose a single one.
So I hope to hand deliver this to you my friend
Face to face
Following a warm embrace.

There is no doubt
I have studied Hannah and Issac's
Situation,
From my point of view,
My perspective .

Chapter 12

Then being enlightened
I have tried desperately
To see these as God's children
Just in my charge.

But what about their perspective,
Their wants and needs,
Hopes and fears,
Of these I know nothing.

I just did what I thought best,
Totally ignoring
Their input,
I am embarrassed.

So my new challenge
Is to ask them.
Guide them
Towards self discovery .

My life is similar
To a patchwork quilt
A multitude of lessons
Sewn together.

They define Abraham Graham
In small pieces,
Patches, extensions.
Slowly I grow.

The Lord's patience is infinite,

For my monumental discoveries ,
Great growth spurts,
Are only minute patches in time.

When I speak to God
It is often I can not find a starting place
And my pitiful brain can not understand
Why my life is so blessed.

Betsy, our farm,
My health, my friend HJ,
The letters,
Amazing authors.

Then Hannah and Issac
And so much more.
I think of Job his trials and tribulations,
I think of Abraham Graham with a blessed life.

Job had so much to learn from,
So much to kindle his growth.
I with so many blessing
Am I untried?

Is my house built on sand?
I pray my faith is strong
Tested
For I love the Lord dearly.

Would it be more of a blessing
To be misused?

Chapter 12

Attacked,
Ground down?

Would a faith born of tribulations
Out weigh a faith born of blessings?
My thoughts turn to the story of the Prodigal Son
And I know not the answer.

Well my friend the train is due
So I must close,
We are on the way!

Your friend
Abraham

Smoking and steaming
The black behemoth
Rolled through the station stoping
It's cat like car tail
By the platform.

Four got off and three got on
Awe and excitement.
Finding seats they got ready
As the man in the uniform
Yelled "alllll aboard!!!!"

There was clanking as the cars stretched out
And the train slowly snaked out into
The Texas country side.

Abraham sat with his back to the engine
Put his head back and closed his eyes
But it was too early,
For Issac's enthusiasm called for
Abraham to look at this and look at that.

So Abraham smiled, nodded,
Mm hummed, and ah uhhed
For the next fifty miles or so
Till the gentle rocking train finally lulled
him to sleep.

It's easier at eight years old
To believe, that is,
Less disappointments,
Faster to trust.

Hannah was here
His sister
In a mother role,
She loved him no doubt.

And the old man,
Hannah said he rescued them
He talked to God a lot,
He loved them.

Then

Heading to her fourteenth year on this earth.
What was Hannah seeing?

Chapter 12

Her brother,
Known all his life,

The back of his tousled head
Over eight years of her life,
Tears, fears, aggravation
Now her responsibility.

And an old man,
A kind stranger,
A benefactor,
An unknown,

A yet to be seen.
He spoke often of God
Seemed kind and fair
He felt safe.

He said he loved her and Issac,
He certainly acted like that.
He was taking them to a big city
He talked to an old mule.

The wind from the open windows
Made the heat bearable.
Every so often a strong smell of coal smoke
Drifted in the windows.

Though the breeze was cooling
And appreciated
Abraham was still sweating,

So he gladly accepted the canteen from Hannah.

Issac grabbed a sandwich
And immediately turned back to
The view of the country side
Rolling past.

Hannah and Abraham said
Grace over the sandwiches,
Some of Hannah's homemade
Pickles
And a large sugar cookie also Hannah-made.

Changing trains in Eastland
They were making good time
So baring unforeseen difficulties
They would be on time.

They were due in Fort Worth
About 9:30 in the evening.
Dr Rainer insisted on meeting them
So Abraham was praying they wouldn't be late.

Abraham reaching a fullness
late afternoon
Felt the need to thank God.
Seems his blessings cup
Was running over.

Watching the children
Still fascinated by the

Chapter 12

Ever changing country side
And lengthening shadows.

Lord I am amazed,
I am humbled,
I am thankful,
I am blessed.

No matter the speed of the train
Darkness still over took them.
The porter came through
Lighting the coal-oil compartment lights.

The wind from the window cooled
As the night came down.
Black dark occasionally broken by
A single farm,
An occasional one with electric lights.

Hannah finally asleep
Curled in the seat,
Head on Abraham's knee.
Issac sprawled over both facing seats
As only an eight year boy can sprawl.

They rocked on through the night
Occasionally passing
Small sleepy towns,
And crossing an occasional bridge.

9:51 by Abraham's watch

They pulled into the Fort Worth
Station.
Truly magnificent,
It was huge!

Hannah and Issac
Were in awe!
Carpet bag in tow they walked slowly
With mouths wide open.

Noise and people everywhere
Even at this time of night.
Abraham had to admit
He was overwhelmed as well.

Mr Graham?
Mr Abraham Graham?
Dr Edgar Rainer at your service sir,
Please call me Edgar.

May I assist you to the car?
And you must be Hannah and Issac,
I have been looking forward
To making your acquaintance.

Tall
Well Dressed,
Very slender
Distinguished ,
Very large smile.

Chapter 12

Abraham immediately felt trust
A liking of this man.
He knew from HJ's earlier letter
This man's impressive position and credentials
But he felt no pride or pretentiousness.

Outside into the streets of Fort Worth
The trio stepped,
Walking up to what appeared to be
A new or newer Buick sedan,
Quite grand indeed.

"Heed wanted to be here to greet you,
But the retirement home
Limits their residents night time outings,
So we will be meeting him for breakfast early
tomorrow morning,

Though based on excitement when we last spoke,
I'm not sure he will sleep much tonight.
He has been waiting so long to put a face
and person
To your magnificent letters.

If you will board the passenger side,
Young people in the back
I will try to get us to my home in one piece.
My house is a bit overwhelming
Now that Carolyn has passed and my family has
grown up and moved out.

I often feel I should move to a smaller domicile
But I so love it when all my children
Come home at one time.
The house is noisy and full
As it should be.

So many stores,
Electric lights,
Street lights,
Then houses.

Tree lined lanes
More electric street lights,
You could still here the crickets
And cicadas,
But almost no frogs.

The house was grand,
What Abraham thought of
When Jesus said "there are many Mansions".
Hannah said it looked like a castle.

When they reached the front door
It was opened by a young man.
He and a young woman
Were introduced as Wade and Celia Rainer
Edgar's youngest son.

"They insisted that I would need help
In getting y'all settled,
So who am I to resist

Chapter 12

Such a beautiful woman.

Wade will take you to your rooms
If you'd like to freshen up,
And Celia has laid out a few snacks
Just in case any one is hungry".

The children plunged up the stairs
While Abraham's was more of a plod.
The indoor bathroom
Was fascinating to Hannah and Issac,
And Abraham was secretly impressed as well.

Then downstairs again and
into the kitchen for a few small cakes
And what Celia called "finger sandwiches".
Abraham waited on Issac for a remark
But he held his counsel.

The children were given a new drink
That Wade and Celia's children loved
It was called "Cool Aid" cherry flavored
They were entranced .

Slowly the two young one began to fade
So it was decided to go to bed for the night.
Abraham was happy too
For he was exceedingly tired himself.

A beautiful bedroom
Right next to the children

The bed springs didn't creak
And the sheets smelled of lilac and sunshine.

My Heavenly Father

What a wonderful day!
A safe trip
Two beautifully behaved children,
The kindest people

And a good safe place to rest.
You generosity knows no bounds
Lead me when I speak to these people
Guard my words.

Help me be a living example of you Lord.
Your humble servant,

Abraham Graham

Chapter 13

Slept heavy!
Like a log
The sky was already lightning up
And coffee was on.

Edgar was reading his Bible
Sipping his coffee
At the kitchen table.
He waved Abraham over and filled his cup.

"Abraham
I must say this
before it slips from
An old man's mind"

Edgar closed his Bible
Sat up in his chair
And said "I'm 69
Met a lot of men in my day.

Some proud some humble,
Honest and evil,
But never have I shaken the hand

Of a harder worker than you.

Your hand, the grip of a fine honest man
feels like shoe leather,
Tough, calloused, from daily hard work,
A fine statement of a man's life.

Your letters to HJ
Have kept me on my toes.
Holding myself up for inspection
Reanalyzing my relationship with my Lord".

Abraham, in unfamiliar surroundings
Was not used to compliments of this nature.
This man was sincere
And a man to be admired, respected.

With some moments of quiet
Abraham said,
"I accept your kind compliment
Sir in the name of our Lord.

For in my 79 years
I haven't found any evidence
To cause myself to feel special,
Or in any other way worthy of being singled out"
Other than, of course, the Lord's love and great sacrifice,

"I have, however often kept the company this one, beyond reproach,

Chapter 13

Of an unassailable nature
A being of perfection.

Being of a meager nature myself,
and easily lost, or confused,
I have found it prudent just to keep my head down,
and watch for his footsteps.

He will not lead me astray.
At no time have I ever been abandoned,
there is always a clear path
To follow.

So, if there is anything to compliment sir
I can assure you, it could only be
From the reflections of my Lord Jesus Christ,
and naught to do with me".

Edgar sat for a moment, staring at his coffee cup,
then smiling as though to himself spoke,
saying " indeed sir indeed."
Then he finished his coffee and said

"If you are ready Abraham,
we can leave the children in the care of Wade
and Celia,
I believe they will be also
Be in the company of several of my grandchildren.
And I know assuredly that HJ is waiting impatiently
to shake your hand, and greet his friend".

Abraham finished his cup and stood saying " I am ready".

An amazing ride, so many automobiles,
Grand houses and buildings of several stories.
It could have been overwhelming,
had he not followed Edgar's cue, and accepted it as normal.

Arriving at the "Nursing home" as HJ called it
Abraham was again impressed by the massive oak trees,
the manicured grounds
And the grand brick structure.

Pulling up to the front steps
And stepping from the car
He saw a man in a white suit rise from his chair on the grand veranda
And walk to the head of the stairs.

Abraham, in clean white shirt and new Levi overalls climbed the stairs
And took the hand of H J Foroon Jr
Author mentor and friend.

The handshake wasn't enough
So the two old men embraced.
There at the top of the stairs
Of The Eventide Baptist retirement Home.

CHAPTER 13

HJ introduced Abraham to all the old men
On the veranda,
And they entered the lobby.
Impressive 30 foot ceilings huge green palms
Shiny marble floors.

An iced water cooler on a stand
With little paper cones as drinking cups
In a dispenser on the side.
Overstuffed leather chairs
Occupied by elderly gentleman with Bibles and
Newspapers.

Edgar said "I will leave you two
To enjoy this time together, Abraham,
I will be available to pick you up when you two
have tired
Though I'm sure it will be quite a while"

They shook hands and Edgar
Made his way out of the Lobby.
HJ, Watching him walk away
Said "such a fine, fine Christian friend"

Abraham replied "truly a fine Christian man".
They made their way to the Eventide dining hall
And enjoyed an excellent breakfast
with general talk of the trip, the children,
and Edgar.

Over the second cup of coffee

Abraham said "oh! I have a letter for you,
I brought it rather than posting
And he pulled the folded paper from his
bib pocket.

HJ laughed and said "I thought to hand deliver
mine as well!"
And reaching inside his white suit jacket,
He pulled forth his letter, which they exchanged
over the table of breakfast remnants.

"I must confess" HJ started "I was unable to fast, as
promised in my letter. It caused great concern
here, and I had to relent, seems it is frowned on by
our resident Doctor and nutritionist.
But I have prayed wholeheartedly"
He smiled

Sipping coffee they read in silence

While HJ read Abraham's letter written in
Aspermont, Abraham was reading:

Abraham
My brother in Christ

You're coming!
I can hardly believe it.
Almost two years we have been corresponding
And I feel as if we have been friends forever,
And I guess with our Lord Jesus Christ

Chapter 13

As our focal point
How could one feel any other way.

It is the Lord who offers our cohesiveness,
Our life's goal
Surely in Christ our brotherhood is confirmed timeless.

To meet with some one who loves and seeks the Lord the
same as I is truly uplifting and encouraging .
Abraham you are living in God's miracle.

I have so much to say
I fear I will gush,
Stammer
As a child.

However knowing you as I do
I fear no judgment,
No criticism,
My friend Abraham Graham

Here at The Eventide
I am truly blessed.
I intend to fast and pray
These last two days before your arrival

In great anticipation.
Your brother in "The Following"
HJ

Upon finishing their reading

They each folded and pocketed their letters.
Refreshed their coffee as the breakfast dishes were
taken away

They sipped coffee in silence
Listening to the muted sounds from the dining
room kitchen
And old men conversing
In the corners.

HJ was very dignified in appearance
But his smile was all joy,
It brightened the room
And made it impossible for you not to smile as well.

More frail than Abraham had hoped
But HJ appeared happy
And safe.
Abraham was impressed with HJ's surroundings.

"It's never good to guess at God's plans"
Abraham said,
"First our mind is to small
 to conceive of what he has in store
 or the convolutions necessary to get there".

"The second is simple
 It just isn't our business.

 Man should know what business is his and
 what is God's

Chapter 13

And stay out of God's business.
So I'll just say, it is truly a wonder to me,
You and I sitting here today
I am alway enriched by following God's plan.

A lesson to be learned over and over."
HJ said
"I was asked to speak to a religion class at Baylor University
When my book was first released.
I was looking forward to an active class
with a spirited question and answer period after.

Not one question or sign of approval.
I went looking to reach forty odd students,
and nothing.
It was ten years later I received a letter
From a Dr. Henderson, telling me how that class had changed his life,
And the revivals he had preached and colleges he had both taught and lectured.

I went for the class, my business,
God called me for Ned Henderson, God's business.
We are so short sighted, small planned.

We do so well when we let God lead
The coffee was cold but the companionship warm,
They adjourned to the veranda to speak to some of HJ's fellow residents.

A beautiful view, retired missionaries
and preachers
All men of God,
The conversations
Heated, convicted.

A fine blessed afternoon
And all to early,
Abraham recognized Edgar's Buick
Pulling into the tree lined drive.

HJ and Abraham said goodbye with an embrace.
Abraham's conversation turned
To Hannah and Issac
And a report of HJ and his conversation
from the day.

The children were full of tales
Of visiting the nearby lake
Feeding ducks
Games with Ben, Alice and Eva.

They were beside themselves
Talking fast and swapping subjects.
They had been invited to the Stockyards
To see some real cowboys and some long-
horn cattle
Tomorrow.

Well Abraham was glad they were having
so much fun

Chapter 13

but to tell the truth
He missed them.
He wished he could sure some time with them.

A delicious evening meal,
And they retired early.
Abraham and the two children
Enchanted and exhausted.

Chapter 14

Second full day in Fort Worth
Abraham wasn't sure why
But he was a might tired.
He'd done no work since they left

Didn't make sense.
Slept like a log last night,
Over slept again this morning
Woke with a funny feeling.

Aloneness, separateness,
Abraham couldn't pray.
Stodgy feeling
Words fell from his lips uninspired, insincere.

Abraham wasn't scared,
Just uncomfortable,
Un-whole,
A new and unwanted feeling.

He knew God was there
Never doubted.
There wasn't anything wrong with God.

So it had to be himself.

So Abraham prayed
A new prayer.
"Most High, king of Kings,
Your Abraham's feeling lost.

Now I know you'd never leave me Lord,
So I musta wandered off.
Can't seem to see my way back this morning.
I would be obliged if you'd shine a light.

Nudge me back into your fold.
I'm am nothing with out you Lord,
Thank you for hearing me, loving me, and
answering my prayer.

In Thy holy name
Amen".

Maybe not clear,
Maybe not normal but a lot safer
Abraham followed clinking dishes
And children's laughter, downstairs.

Edgar was in the midst of explaining
Something to Issac and a black haired child about
Issac's age.
They both were giggling and Edgar had a broad
grandfather's grin.

Chapter 14

"Look Abraham! Look what I've laid out before you!
Blessings galore,
Love abundant,

I will never abandon you"
Tears and laughter from Abraham
As he walked into the room
Edgar turned and seeing his tears said,

"Are you well my friend?"
Abraham smiled broadly saying,
"I was touched by this beautiful sight
God is so gracious".

Edgar smiled and said "Indeed my friend indeed".
Turning back to the boys
Edgar finished his tale.

HJ's men's group
Was meeting that evening
To visit with Abraham.
Edgar had mentioned they were excited

He thought about it and wondered
If he should be nervous or apprehensive,
He rejected those feelings
For it would not be Abraham there,
For he was the Lord's representative.

The young black haired child was Theodore
One of Edgar's younger grandchildren.

They were all excited about the stockyards.
And he was confident in the safety of the children.

Time with Edgar was so fulfilling
Such a sincere wise man,
Unassuming
He felt he could not get enough of Edgar in the
time he had.

God was showing Abraham something,
Offering a time of learning.
For the children,
For the church.

God would reveal the purpose when it was right
Or never
Either one is alright.

The automobile ride to see HJ was as exciting and
amazing as before,
So much to take in
So much never seen before.

I am so tiny Lord
How can you see me?
Why would you see me,
How big a love does that take?

HJ was waiting on the veranda
Gracious, dressed all in white.
He embraced Abraham

Chapter 14

They nodded and waved their way inside.

They both had a muffin, butter,
And some fresh black coffee.
HJ, after a short silence,
Spoke with his soft Texas drawl.

"Friends
Being a man of virtually no family
I find a few close friends
Are my only family.

Not a brilliant or new observation
But factual, and since they are an informed
and personally selected group, I value each and
everyone highly.
Abraham my brother, there are none closer
than you".

"A true an honor my friend" replied Abraham
"My family is small, Hannah, Issac, and yourself.
I have friends but none near as close as you three".

"I have something I need help with HJ"
Said Abraham,
This morning I became disoriented,
Not physically but spiritually.

I felt a separation from my Lord.

I did not doubt Him, it was as if I could reach out as far as I could and still not touch God. As if He were beyond my voice.
Knowing He is a constant, I had to postulate that it was I that had strayed."

Knowing nothing else, I prayed
"Most High, king of Kings,
Your Abraham is feeling lost.

Now I know you'd never leave me Lord,
So I must have wandered off
Can't seem to find my way back.

I should would be appreciative
of your guidance,
were you to light my way home.

Nudge me back into your fold,
For I'm am nothing with out you.
Thank you for hearing me, Loving me, and answering my prayer.

In Thy holy name
Amen"

HJ said "I have on occasion felt removed from the Lord as well. I also agree,
It is none of the Lords doings.
However, I have chosen to try and be aware of the workings of satan.

Chapter 14

A true Christian is a pox in the devil's life, and often a prime target.
What ever the reason your prayer was the answer to that distance"

Abraham listened intently,
becoming aware of how little he thought of and watched for the devil.
Perhaps that was the opening that Satan needed, unawareness, complacency.

Abraham, silent for a few minutes
Said " I have known Satin to be a tempter
and a worker in half light, and part truths,
but I admit I have not thought of him often,
or been vigilant in my defenses.
I guess you could say I am a prime target for an attack".

Abraham continued "also today
I was struck by mankind's diminutive statue in such a massive universe!
Making God's love and sacrifice for us the greater.
That an omnipotent being this Grand would still be aware of, love,
And care for Abraham Graham, is beyond human understanding.
It could only be contributed to a Godly love.
1 John 4:16 explains it when saying
God is Love, there could be no other explanation".

The afternoon passed too swiftly, evening meal as a guest of HJ's,
They, coffee cups in hand, adjourned to a small meeting room just off of the main dining hall.
Edgar was just arriving.

They arrived.
Such an impressive group,

Reverend Byron Stewart, Pastor of Fort Worth Calvary, Dr. Edgar Rainer, Department Head of Theology, South Western Baptist Theological Seminary, Father Liam McAnderson, Rector of The Church of St Thomas, William Franklin, Department Head of The School of Educational Ministries, South Western Seminary, Reverend Horace Dobkins, Trinity Methodist Church, Reverend Samuel P. Framton, Pastor, Bethal Lutheran Church.
Abraham was introduced individually to Byron, Liam, William, Horace, Samual, Edgar and HJ of course he knew.

Coffee was poured, a couple of pipes appeared, some familiar banter as everyone found a comfortable chair.
After a lot of hand shaking and exchanged greeting a short silence and Byron Stewart said " Well Abraham I'm sure I speak for all of us when I say we are glad to put a face to the letters HJ's shared with us.

Chapter 14

We have thoroughly enjoyed the contents fueling many discussions and initiating several new lines of thought.

All here being followers of the Lord Jesus Christ often find ourselves in search of a better understanding of our own personal relationship with Him.

I can speak for myself when saying your letters have helped me greatly.
Whereupon there were numerous "here here's" heard in the room.
Then a silence.

Abraham started "if I may I'd like to tell you of my last few days.
It is with great excitement and no small amount of trepidation I have anticipated the meeting with you August gentlemen.
HJ's and my friendship has grown over this last year to a brotherhood.

Trusting HJ as I do I felt assured of safety however it has not been as easy to quell my feelings of inferiority.

After considerable prayer and no small battle with self, I finally realized,
This is not a meeting of titled men and a self educated farmer.

But a meeting of followers of Christ
(Amens, smiles and much nodding)
If I am here to speak as Abraham I have
come in vain,
If I am here to listen with Abraham's ears I am deaf.

So may I say I consider we a band of brothers,
searchers for Christ and my ears are open."
Abraham was silent, they all were.

If I brought something
I would say it is confusion,
A lack of ability to see
Where self stops and God's will starts.

I so often find myself
Wandering between self and God's will
Blind to my crossing over from God to self.

I have heard it spoken of
Crucifixion of self,
Oh that I could attain that plateau,
But I remain torn between the two.

God's eternal grace my only value,
I trust as Christian men
You will forgive my slips into self,
And gently point them out.

Abraham was quiet again

Chapter 14

Edgar spoke up, "with Abraham's permission
I would tell you of my past two days spent with
Abraham, Hannah and Issac."
And he continued at length.

The meeting went on well into the night leaving
Edgar and Abraham to ride home in relative
silence. So much said so much love for the Lord. So
much to ponder.

Abraham and the children were to start their
return trip in the morning
Leaving to catch the 10:14 to Sweetwater, and
changing for Aspermont and home.

The children were asleep when Edgar and
Abraham arrived home, shaking hands and
thanking the Lord for such a blessed day they
went to bed.

Abraham woke at 5:30 and after dressing and
packing went downstairs
For coffee.
Edgar was up, the family cook already hard at work
with what appeared to be an inordinately large
breakfast.

Guests started arriving just before 6:00
And by 6:20 all were present including HJ.
Such a send off, Abraham was again moved to tears.
But this morning Hannah and Issac were the stars.

A few brightly wrapped gifts lots of conversations
with the children and Edgar soon announced the
departure time had arrived.
Goodbyes said, hand shaking and a few embraces,
the three waved goodbye from Edgars car window.

Saying goodbye to Edgar was hard.
He had turned out to be a good friend.
He said his house would be quiet and empty,
And Abraham remembered what that was like.

The train ride was different, the first two hours
were tales of Hannah and Issac's exploits. All about
their new friends and what they planned when
they got home.
Sandwiches and milk packed by Martha, Edgars
cook, who turned out to be one of their favorites.

Slowly the excitement the food and the gentle
rocking of the train brought on silence
As the train rolled into the twilight lit Texas
countryside.

Leaving Abraham alone with his thoughts
and prayers.

"My Lord Jesus

Why me, you bless me so.
I am at a loss, there is so much to say and
much to ask.

Chapter 14

Right now I am overwhelmed with ideas, questions, experiences.
Such a rich gift. I ask to be lead by you.
What to glean and understand from this visit.
I thank you Lord please help me be a better servant.

In Jesus name
Amen

Chapter 15

Home!
They changed trains in Eastland,
Reaching Aspermont by 2:00 in the afternoon.
Newt was out of town,
But the truck started right up.

The three Grahams pulled into the drive by 4:00.
The all agreed it was a comforting sight.
Not fancy like Edgars
But safe.

Glad to be home Hannah and Issac ran to see
the animals
And check the garden.
Abraham was feeling his age a little
And after unpacking,
Sat and watched the sunset.

Hannah took a fresh ham from the smoke house,
Some grits and beans and they sat
Round the kitchen table.
Issac said the blessing

"Lord Jesus
This is Issac Graham,
We're home,
Fort Worth sure was something,

Thank you for keeping us safe,
Thank you for this good food,
Bless Hannah and Abraham,
And that's all,
In the name of Jesus
Amen".

It was a fine meal
Everybody pitched in to clean up
And they called it an early night.
A few minutes of creaking bed springs
And the house was silent.

Abraham rose first
Still dark and quiet he went
Quietly into the kitchen
Lit some kindling,

And sat down at the table.
It was a long trip,
Harder than he thought
Every bone and muscle he had
Ached.

There was a time that trip would've
Been no big step for a stepper,

Chapter 15

But Abraham has come to realize of late
He was now more of a plodder,
A shuffler you might say.

No regrets, no wish I weres,
Now more thankful,
More amazed at God's gifts
Blessed beyond deserving.

HJ now a warm feeling place in his heart,
Much like an older brother.
The coffee boiled and he poured a cup
And sat back down.

The house was spotless
As the night gave way to the dawn.
He noticed the garden gate wasn't sagging,
Issac and he were gonna fix that when
they got back.

The children were tuckered
No need for early rising.
The chores would wait
As the early sun turned the farm to gold
and greens.

Abraham walked out on the back porch
Listening to the birds and Othello tuning up,
Announcing a new day.
Another of the many gifts of God.

"Lord, I am speechless.
There are times a man needs to hush,
To gaze in awe at the uncountable wealth you offer
on a daily basis.
Forgive we poor blind creatures,

Greens, golds, browns,
Yellow blooms on squash plants,
Red roses along the wall
Where Betsy had planted them,
To be seen today.

Not a weed in the garden any where!
Down at the barn
Stalls spotless,
Chicken pen raked.

What in the world?
Tilman couldn't have had time to do all this,
Not and keep his own farm up,
Abraham was truly puzzled.

Jeroboam was glad to se Abraham
And of course an apple,
And a sugar cube or two.
He didn't show it, but Abraham could tell.

What was it about that old feller?
That almost snow white face?
The deep brown eyes?

Chapter 15

Or maybe the bond two make when they've both
known hard work.

What ever it was
Abraham's heart was touched
At the smell and the feel of those long ears,
Thank you once more Lord.

Back to the house there was a clanking of
stove doors
And there was a sleepy eyed Hannah,
Going about breakfast fixin's.

With almost nothing to do around the farm
At least nothing pressing
Abraham decided they should go see the Tilman's.

Issac stumbled into the kitchen
Sleepy eyed as well.
They sat down to a fine "Hannah"
Breakfast.
Hannah said grace
And Abraham told of his morning with God.

Very quiet morning ,
Issac was reading a book
Given to him by Edgars grandson.
It was a Horatio Alger adventures,
And Hannah was crocheting.

Fresh tomato and left over bacon sandwiches

Fresh cool tea
And they piled in the truck for a quick visit with the Tilman's

Mr Tilman was down by the creek
Pulling a couple of stumps,
Mrs Tilman said he'd be back directly.
Hannah told her all about Fort Worth,

And in a little while Mr Tilman arrived,
Stomp-in' mud off his boots on the porch.
He came in, had a dipper of well water
And sat down at the table.

Abraham started in to thanking him for all the things he'd done
And Mr Tilman held up a heavily calloused hand
saying "whoa whoa hold your horses",

Gotta tell you,
Things got a little busy round here.
A while back I traded that Finnegan boy
A sickly little calf.
Told him, if he could save him
He'd owe me a weeks work,
If not just two days.

Well that calf turned into a 300 pound heifer
And I asked him to take care of your place for me.
He was down to your place dawn to dusk.

Chapter 15

Never seen a boy work that hard,
'Course he did owe me,
But I reckon it also had sompin'
To do with him taking a shine to your Hannah girl too".

Abraham looked at Hannah
Whose head was bowed and red cheeked.
Abraham moved on "well however or why-ever he is certainly to be commended.

What's his name?"
"Bartholomew but his family call him Barth" Hannah said.
"But I just barely know him we met at church,

He is older than me he'll be 15 in September .
,
He has two pigs and a cow of his own
His father is going to give him thirty five acres when he turns 18.
Then realizing she said to much she
Got quiet.

Abraham looked at the Tilman's with an amused smile and said " Well I can see you don't know much about him".
Hannah blushed deeper and turned to her crocheting.

Abraham talked of the big houses, street lights,

large number of automobiles, indoor bathrooms,
And how nice the folks were.

But also how thankful he was to be home,
And how blessed they felt.
Abraham spokes a little of how important God was
in the lives of the men he had met with,
And the joy at seeing his friend HJ for the first time.

Soon time to start for home he again thanked Mr
Tilman and said their goodbyes.
They drove home .
Hanna had bread to bake,
And Issac had evening chores.

After supper and cleanup
They all listened to the radio.
Abraham and Hannah agreed
On one song they both liked.
Abraham because it was about cows,

Issac just liked it,
And Hannah because the singer was dreamy.
"The last round up" sung by a young feller named
Gene Autry
They say he was in the moving pictures too.

Prying Issac's book out of his hands for bed
wasn't easy
But finally the two were asleep.
Abraham got paper and pencil

Chapter 15

And sat at the kitchen table.

Pencil tip to tongue he began.

Well my Dear Dear friend

It was far too short of a time
Though I'm not sure there would ever be enough.
Truly an important moment in my life
To visit with you and your friends.

Amazing thinkers and Christian men
An honor and privilege to make their acquaintance.
So much to think on ponder
Today watching the sunrise over my small farm
I realized the value of the saying by
Margret Hungerford
"Beauty is in the eye of the beholder"

My farm shone like gold,
Sparkled took away my breath.
Blessed far beyond my understanding,
And especially beyond my deservedness.

What do I do for my Lord?
Little of value,
Naught to "earn" such rewards,
I am in awe.

I have decided to offer Bible schooling
To Hannah and Issac.

It is not that we don't already
Read and learn,
But at a deeper level.

I will not make it mandatory,
Just offer it if they are interested.
Based on the world today and these turbulent times, I feel
it would be strengthening, protective.

When a Christian man's realm of influence is smaller,
Must he not re-evaluate every relationship
To make sure he is spreading Gods word to his
fullest ability?

My audience of two
I can offer more.
We shall see
A test for all three of us.

Your brother
Abraham

Sleep came deep and quick
For Abraham
Knowing he could only teach what he knew.
He would lean heavily on the Lord as always.

Saturday morning at breakfast
He spoke,
"In praying and discussing with HJ
About what I can do for you,

Chapter 15

There is one thing I have not offered you both.

So I will make an offer,
It is up to you to decide,
I will not think less of you or be disappointed
if you are not interested.

Know that I love you,
Am full to bursting with pride
In your behavior, character
And your accomplishments.

I have decided to offer an in depth Bible study,
Sunday mornings before Church.
More than we would cover in Bible school.

It will require study, reading and prayer.
The Lord has blessed me so much,
You two being some of my greatest blessings,
I felt like I should share what I know,
But remember only if you want.

Pray about it,
Think about it,
Talk to each other.
It will be quite an undertaking ,

When you both have a decision
Let me know."
They were quiet, nodded
Finished breakfast

And cleaned up.
Morning chores called
And Abraham felt a need to visit
With Jeroboam.
Taking Jeroboam's harness
He lead him from his stall.

Ears ever alert,
They walked towards the woods.
Abraham had decided to clean
A little under growth and dead wood out.

Never to early to add to the wood pile
Or make the wooded area less prone to fire.
Abraham was quiet for a while,
Choosing his words and thoughts carefully.

"Jeroboam,
I am in search of the Lords purpose for me.
Am I doing everything I can?
Do I sin unawares?
Callously?

I know I lie,
It slips from my tongue
Almost unnoticed.
A false compliment,

Sometimes to avoid personal embarrassment.
Vanity when it comes to God's two children,
Though I know they are the Lord's.

Chapter 15

No need to steal,
Time has taken care of lust,
Only a fool would claim to be sin free.
So,
Doubt?

Judging?
Jeroboam,
Of that I am guilty.
There lies one of my imperfections,
In all putridness.

Now there's a nice big dead oak
Longing to be pulled back to the wood yard.
To provide us cooking and coming winter warmth

Stand still old man while I chain it up,
A light weight
And easy load
For us both."

Pulled back near the barn,
Abraham started lopping off branches
Making a brush pile.
Good for kindling.

He getting ready to saw
When Issac walked up,
"May I help with the sawing?"
Abraham stared with pride.

Not of self,
Of this nine year old young man.
He was thankful for the offer
Of company, as much as labor.

"My dear Issac I would be honored".
Issac grabbed the two man saw,
Abraham put up the one man saw
And they began the push pull.

In awhile Hannah appeared,
Two thick slices of homemade bread
Slathered in fresh butter,
The three paused.

Tree stump perched,
Soon licking buttered fingers,
Hannah said "Issac
Will you speak now?"

Issac wiped his hands on the dish towel
Hannah had wrapped his bread in
And began.

"Abraham, father
We are amazed at your wisdom
Your dedication to our Lord.
Because we are children doesn't mean
We are unaware.

We both would be honored to learn

Chapter 15

More of Gods word
From such a man as you,
From Hannah and I it is "yes please".

Abraham stood, mouth open
Who was that?
Surely not little Issac!
Speaking like that!

Touched
He could not stop the tears
They both came to him
Took a hand each
And leaned into their Abraham,
Their father.

Chapter 16

Lord Jesus Christ

I am tasked
With reading and explaining your words to
your children.
What audacity, impossible for Abraham Graham.

Only you,
Your voice,
Your knowledge,
It is the most daunting of assignments.

I must not allow self participation!
I will do my best
To repeat only your words,
Use me.

In the name of The Lord Jesus Christ,
Your humble farmer
Abraham

The Bible Study began 8:00 Sunday morning.
Hannah and Issac walked into the parlor,

Bibles, tablets and pencils in hand.
They sat ready

Abraham sat down,
"Well
I have prayed much of the night
To be the best conveyor of God's voice.
Please pray for me.

Issac will you read the first chapter of Genesis "
When Issac had finished
Abraham asked, "tell me what you read and heard"
And the children spoke of the light, the land, the
world and it's living creatures
That God created.

Abraham said, "As the creator of this
There may be a different view.
In God's wisdom He created Man in His own image
And the earth as our dwelling place.

Much as we would create a place for some one or
something we loved.

"When we three build a pen and shelter
for our pigs,
It is for their welfare, their safety,
It is because we care for them.

The goats see the water,
They see the shelter,

Chapter 16

The food trough, the grass.
,
The fences enclose them
A cover to avoid rain or sun,
A place they will know,
Their world.

What do we, as the builders, see?
A place to keep them safe from coyotes and wolves,
To keep them safe from wandering,
Provided because of our caring,

Concern for their well being,
Food, protection,
A growing space,
A gift.

We see farther, we see more.
We know they will give milk,
Cheese, and multiply.
We are their caretakers.

How much more does our God know,
How much more does He See?"

If we see only what is in front of us
We have missed God's real gifts."
Abraham continued.

The hour was soon over.
They finished dressing and piled into the truck

For church.

Abraham thought as he drove,
"Lord I hope you are pleased with my words,
I know naught without Your revelations,
Guide me Lord.

Strangely enough,
This Sunday's message was brought by
Aaron Finnegan,
Barth's father
A strong soft-spoken man.

It was a good message
Leaving Abraham with food for thought.
Next Sunday was decided upon to be an all
day affair,
With several messages and dinner on the grounds.

Mr Finnegan and his son Bartholomew
Came up and introduced themselves after
the service,
Hannah kept her head down
But Abraham noticed her blushing.

Barth, as he was called
Kept his head down too.
Abraham praised his work
To him and his father both.

Chapter 16

Mr. Finnegan said " my son has something he
wishes to ask of you"
Barth said " sir, Issac and Hannah have told me of a
Bible study
you are leading for them, and I was wondering if I
could be allowed to attend?"

Abraham responded with a yes,
And dealing with Mr Finnegan,
Arranged the Bible study to start at 8:30
Sunday mornings
in the church building.

Mr Finnegan told Abraham,
"My son Bartholomew is a serious young man
for his age,
A hard worker, Bible reader, honest,

And though I expect this request to be partially
motivated by your daughter Hannah's presence,
I feel sure I can promise a dedicated
Student in whom you will not be disappointed."

The ride home was full of talk and plans for the
dinner on the grounds Sunday.
God is so good
Abraham spent most of the ride home in prayer
and thanksgiving.

Monday.;
Aspermont, supplies,

Post office to mail a letter and receive
Five letters!
HJ, Dr E Rainer, Rev S.P. Framton, and Rev Dobkins
The fifth letter being addressed to Mr Issac
Graham from Mr. Benjamin Rainer.

Abraham felt rich, wealthy,
So many friends
He felt overwhelmed.
He was anxious to return home
And read his letters.

Though HJ's being the most important,
All were welcome now that he could put voices and
faces to the names..

On the way home, Issac tried hard to read his
letter from Ben
But the bouncing in and out of the ruts
Made it too difficult

Arriving home
There were chores, lunch,
And then time for letters.
Abraham sat at the kitchen table with a new oil-
cloth table cloth
Bluebonnets on a white background.

Paid for out of Hannah's egg money,
Right out of the Sears and Roebuck Catalog.
She was proud to be contributing to

Chapter 16

The household.

Abraham was also proud
So thankful to God.
True there was the occasional
Wistfulness when he wished Betsy here.
She would always be his better half.

She would have loved the children so!
They were a true comfort to Abraham.
He thought it strange that he had not known he was lonely until he wasn't.

Sliding the blade of his freshly honed Barlow
under the flap
Of the first letter,
He could hear HJ's voice and he had to smile.

My Dear, dear, Abraham

What a visit what a glorious worshipful time!
I sit where we sat, close my eyes
And you sit across from me,

Drinking coffee, and speaking of our Heavenly Father!
I do hope your and the children's trip home was pleasant.

Edgar spoke in detail of yours and his conversations.
Your thoughts sparked several deep discussions
But above all we all enjoyed your visit.

I have a special request.
Your letters have meant so much to
Us all,
Surely God would be in favor of
Letting others learn from these letters.

I would like your permission to correlate your letters,
Perhaps create a small book with you has the author.
Not for your glory at all for I know you would not
want that,
But sharing your insights regarding our Lord.

I have been thinking.
I try to figure out God's plan,
As if I would understand,
As if it's any of my business.

When it comes to my life
I am short sighted.
I speculate and guess
But I don't know.

My only job
Is to live as Christ-like as possible.
This moment, this minute, this hour,
Today
I can do no more.

I guess it's human nature to want to know why.
It takes a stronger faith to trust God implicitly
And step out on the waves,

Chapter 16

Knowing he will hold you up.

Such a grand visit!
God bless you Abraham Graham

HJ

Publish his letters?
Not something he wanted,
But if they were given to him by God
He could not refuse to share.

But they would be worthless without HJ's as well.
Silly thought
Nothing would come of it.

Edgar's letter next

Mr Dear Abraham

A wonderful meeting, a wonderful
Visit.
My house still echoes with the sounds of children's voices
Such a blessing.
Hannah and Issac! such grand young people!

It was an honor.
I already miss our morning talks.
I hope you will be able to come again,
My house is your house

You three are always welcome.

Your friend in Christ
Edgar

Issac came into the kitchen to tell of Ben's letter,
This was Issac's first letter ever and he was feeling
very important,
And more than a little excited

Evening chores called
Issac and Abraham and they headed for the barn,
As Hannah made notes about what she
intended to cook
For Sunday's dinner on the grounds.

She was going to get Mrs Tilman to help her perfect
her fried chicken.
Not something she liked to do,
Killing chickens,
But she had heard Barth loved fried
Chicken.

Issac and Abraham laughed at the antics of
the piglets
And talked about the possibilities
Of Issac earning enough money for a 22 rifle.

Issac explained about all the rabbits and squirrels
He could contribute to the dinner table,

Chapter 16

Though not whether Hannah would cook
them or not.

As the sun set they headed for the kitchen.
Great smells
Home, love,
God is so good.
With the children bedded
It was time for Rev Dobkins
And Rev Framton's letters.
Abraham unfolded his Barlow.

Dear Abraham

A true pleasure and blessing
Your dedication to our Lord is apparent.
I would have loved to spend more time with you.
Thank you so much for allowing
HJ to share your letters.

We are all hoping you will be able to visit again and
perhaps a little longer.
Your friend
Saul Framton

Kind soft spoken man
He remembered him because
He felt during their meeting that Saul was
watching him
Very closely

His handshake and comments seemed
very genuine

Then he opened Rev Dobkins
Letter

Dear Abraham

Thank you so much for your visit.
I have enjoyed your letters
And your life experiences.
Truly God sought out the right man
To mentor his children Hannah and Issac.

If you can schedule a return visit
Would you consider speaking to my
Congregation?
We would be honored to pay for train fare
For you and the children.
Again may say it was a very real pleasure.

Your brother in Christ

Well It would be a while if not forever,
For Abraham to want to go that far by train again.
That train ride was to hard on this eighty year
old farmer.

It was getting late,
The coal oil lamp was getting low
And starting to smoke,

Chapter 16

Time to turn in,

But he needed to talk.

It was a ritual now,
The kitchen table.
Though the light was smokier tonight,
Just a quick letter to HJ.

My Brother.
Dignified,
White suited,
Wise worded,
God inspired,
Friend.

HJ

Its is I, your country cousin Abraham.

I received letters from Edgar, Saul, and Horace.

Horace asked me to consider a return trip
they would like me to speak to his church
And even offered to pay our train tickets.

The trip was hard on me
Since we are closer to age I feel you can understand that,
So I immediately thought to myself
I won't be taking that trip again.

*But then again I have to remember
That's Gods business,
And there goes Abraham
Jumping right in the middle of it once more.*

*I need to hear more of the snares
And traps of Satan.
It is not that I am totally unaware,
But he is the king of subtleties.*

*They slip through
The half truths,
That turn us from our course
Without our noticing.*

*Were the devil to tell me
The sky were red instead of Blue,
I would laugh and call him a fool.
But if the devil said "does not the sky have a slight reddish tint today?*

*I might look hard and imagine it so.
For we humans
Are such susceptible creatures,
Easily lead.
Did not the Lord Himself refer to us as sheep?*

*Fore-warned is fore-armed.
I am surprised at how
I have ignored satan,
I'm sure he was pleased.*

Chapter 16

I will renew my prayer
Taking into account
A Christian is always under attack,
For ever, a prey.
Share with me your wisdom,
For I have been lulled into a false sense of safety.
I await your advice

Your friend
Abraham

Sealing the envelope,
He placed it on the parlor table
To be mailed
On the next trip to Aspermont.

Headed for bed
His tired was deeper,
His recovery was slower,
As the bed springs sang their nightly song.

Abraham began,

Heavenly Father
Where do I start?
So much to be thankful for.

So much to see,
So much to feel,
So much love and friendship!
I truly am a wealthy man.

Yet I have been naive,
Been un-vigilant,
Blind to Satan!
I have left Your children unguarded.

Guide me Lord,
Protect us,
Bless us.

Your servant
Abraham.

Chapter 17

A trip to the loft
Sparked by a single gold leaf,
Drifting down,
A seasonal tap on the shoulder.

A whisper of fall.
Hinted at
By a drifter,
The first of many.

Taking out his bandana
Abraham dusted off the chair and sat.
So much as happened in these last three years.

Most of all
Abraham felt he had grown much closer to God.
Less academic,
More as a child to father relationship.

So much more social contact,
Church members
Newt, the men's group,
HJ and of course the children.

No more falling leaves,
Issac was banging on the slop bucket
Calling the pigs to eat.
Jeroboam was standing by his
Feed bucket expectantly.

Mrs Tilman was in the kitchen teaching Hannah
A new way to fry up a hen.
Issac began practicing with his sling shot,
You could hear the bang
Every time he hit that old pie pan
he'd nailed to the fence post.

A wonderful time
To be alive.
It was great in the loft
But he worried about the climbing down.

Abraham had been thinking lately
About Hannah and Issac's future.
He felt guilty but he was hoping
Something might develop
Between Barth and Hannah.

They were far to young for marriage,
But it would be nice to know
She had someone who loved her.
The children would of course inherit the farm.

He thought he'd write HJ after supper.
Abraham knew God would provide

Chapter 17

He just needed to know what he should do
for his part.
Of course prayer and patience
Would let him know.

Abraham had also been praying
About his next Bible study.
Strangely enough
It was dealing with satan in the serpent form.

Hannah had used all her new skills
Working so hard,
Fried chicken, mashed potatoes
Black eyed peas and fresh yeast rolls!
Abraham and Issac were willing
To be practiced on as long as she wanted to.

The night was slightly cooler
But the crickets were still in full voice.
Hannah and Issac tucked in bed,
Abraham got his paper and pencil.

Since the visit, he always saw HJ in his white suit.
It was a great picture as he prepared to write
his letter,
I nice memory
And it caused him to smile as he licked the
pencil point.

My Dear friend HJ

All is quiet here.
The Lord is being patient with me,
As I try to learn not to worry about the children's future,

It's God's and the children's business.
I'm I weak?
Betraying God by worrying about their future?

I'm sure we've addressed this before
But it still comes down to a child's faith
I still don't have.
I worry first then trust God second.
As if I thought I could do anything about the future.

When do we lose it
At what age do we give up that faith?
When do we leap from the garden wall,
Knowing father will be their with outstretched arms.

Then one day we hesitate to leap.
Afraid of falling,
No longer trusting,
When do we start doubting?

I fear my faith
Is specific.
Only when I have no choice
Do I rely on faith.

Chapter 17

As we have discussed before
We know nothing
Of the obstacles he has cleared from our path,
The dangers averted.
It takes a truly great God
To forgive me as often
As I make it necessary.
I am in awe of God Almighty.

Now that you and I have shaken hands,
Sipped coffee,
And come to agreement about our Lord,
I miss you my friend even more.

May the Lord bless you

Abraham

The bed springs sang
A familiar tune.
Deep sleep brought back Betsy for a visit.
Beautiful blue eyes and such a loving smile
She was happy for Abraham
And the children.

He awoke to the sounds of breakfast
And for a moment he thought it Betsy.
Then remembered,
Smiled to himself and thankful for the visit,
Drew his chair up to the table as Hannah poured his coffee.

Hannah wanted to talk about Barth.
She hinted around
Touch on him lightly,
Then moved on to Sunday and dinner on
the grounds.

Abraham listen nodded smiled
Let her take her time.
She was a wise 15 year old
And he knew she would let God guide her.

Issac was going hunting
with his sling shot after breakfast.
He did drop a few hints about being old enough
For a 22 though.

Abraham was caught up on all his chores,
Leaving him to read from the "Screwtape Letters"
For some help preparing for the third chapter
of Genesis.

Friday past well
Even blessed.
Hannah made a large bowl of popping corn
And all were happy around the radio.

There was a different air at Saturday
Breakfast,
There was something up.
Hannah was quiet
Issac and Abraham were normal.

Chapter 17

Abraham watched and listened
And soon realized,
Hannah had to kill two of her chickens today.
Mrs Tilman supplied the last chicken
Now it was Hannah's job.

Tomorrow she had to take her fried chicken
To the church service.
Against Abraham's advice,
All of Hannah's "girls" were named

It was a long day,
Quiet,
Sad.
He watched from the barn just before dusk

As Hannah head to the chicken pen.
She brought two hens back,
Put one under the wash tub,
Chopped off Abigail's head,
Then Nettie.

Abraham went down to the house,
Sat on the backs steps beside Hannah
Put his arm 'round her shoulders
And let her cry as Nettie ran round the
yard headless.

It was a quiet supper.
Hannah bagged all of Abigail and Nettie's feathers
And hung the bodies in the well house

For tomorrow's frying.

Then she went to bed early,
Leaving Issac and Abraham time for man talk.
Issac ask about Abraham when he was young,
And of course the 22 came up.

Hannah was up early
Lighting the stove filling the house with the smell of fried chicken
And yeast rolls.
A good night sleep and excitement about dinner on the grounds
Had gone a long way towards salving last nights sacrifices.

Eggs, bacon, and pan toasted
Halved yeast rolls with butter,
Made Issac and Abraham happy.
Dressed and packed they set off for church.

Arriving at church Hannah put her food in the church foyer,
Abraham found Barth and two of his sisters waiting
For the Bible study.
Becka and Mary asked if they might attend,
And Abraham said they were of course welcome.

After a prayer lead by Barth,
Abraham asked Hannah to read the third chapter of Genesis.

Chapter 17

He then asked them all for interpretations
And thoughts.

The snake was generally believed to be Satan.
Words like mean, scary, evil, we're used
Then Abraham spoke.
"Remember this, Satan does not wish to be recognized.
He is described in the Bible as an angel of light
He speaks in confusion and halve-truths.
He will not identify himself you.

Your best and only defense
Is the Lord, His word.
When you know Him
You will recognize satan for who he is.

They read many Bible verses
Describing the devil,
HIs powers, his ploys,
The real and ever-present danger that
Beelzebub poses.

Mary lead the closing prayer
And they all headed outside,
To talk before going to Sunday School.
From the foyer the church was filled with delicious smells.

A new member of the church was introduced,
A Reverend Dugger.

A 94 year old retired Preacher.

Rev. Dugger had moved in with the Edwards,
Mrs Edwards being his daughter.
He was a Baptist preacher
Known for his fire and brimstone sermons.

The small congregation grew.
The sermon this Sunday was brought by
Mr Henson.
He spoke of Gods love and compassion
for the blind, sick and broken hearted.

The service was a might short,
Maybe due to the delicious smells.
The homemade tables under the trees were
soon filled.
Barth sat across from Hannah
And Abraham wasn't sure anybody
Else got any of Hannah's chicken or rolls.
That boy sure could eat fried chicken and rolls
Hannah blushed and beamed.

Everyone was full of stories and talk driving home.
It was agreed it would be a Sunday to remember
The evening passed swiftly
And beds were soon filled.

An early trip to Aspermont
Was fueled by a fine breakfast
An early morning rain made the ruts treacherous

Chapter 17

But they made it.
Hannah, grocery list in hand and Issac,
22 on his mind, headed for the mercantile.

Abraham headed for the post office....two letters!

HJ and Edgar

Reading HJ's letter he sat on the bench
In front of the mercantile.

Abraham my Dear friend

Your letters mean so much
And you are right
The meeting
Only intensified the caring.

The Christians cross is no doubt
Lack of faith,
Our ultimate failure.
The Lord gave His life for our sins,

And we worry about being fed!
Clothes for the cold,
Water to drink,
Being alone.

We humans all fall short when it comes to faith.

Children are not as familiar with disappointment,

Not accustomed to failure,
Not predisposed to expect the worse,
These are adult maladies.

Inhibiting growth,
Crippling joy,
We label them as
"Just being realistic",
"Facing the facts".

Fear,
The enemy of faith.
Afraid to trust,
Afraid of being hurt.

Does not our father stand
without out-stretched arms
Offering, protection,
A soft place to land?

Our actions
must be prayed over,
We must be vigilant
In prayer for direction.

Our father will not fail us!

It is hard to believe
It's been 9 months since your visit.
I have thought of so much I should have said,
So much undone.

Chapter 17

My dear dear friend,
If we part before another meeting,
Know you revived and old man's faith,
Rescued me from loneliness.

Our friendship as afforded me
Deep joy and fulfillment.
God is wise
For I didn't know how much
I longed for this Friendship.

Your Brother
HJ

Eyes welling up,
Abraham folded the letter,
Put it back in the envelope,
And slid it in to his bib overall pocket.

He would save Edgars for home,
There was much to think about after
HJ's letter.

The children were happy.
The rain still came down
More like a mist.
Almost a fall day, but still a little too warm.

Abraham could not take
These two people for granted.
They shown, sparkled,

Fascinated him.

Hannah was staring out the window,
Issac had fallen asleep with his head in
Abraham's lap,
The sight quickened his heart.

"My Great and Generous Jehovah
What an honor, a blessing,
a responsibility of these two glorious lives
In my care!
I did not know I was lonely, I thought
myself finished.

Thank you Lord for your generosity and wisdom

Amen

The house was a welcome sight,
Well cared for thanks to the two children.
Truly a safe and blessed home
Could a man want more?

Chores done,
A delicious meal,
The Life of Riley,
The Bell Telephone hour,
Gathered 'round the radio
Then bed.

Abraham sat at the table

Chapter 17

And opened Edgars letter.

Greetings my Friend

Forgive me for this letter is to break a confidence
With good intentions.
In the past 9 months,
HJ's health has started to deteriorate .

He asked us not to mention it,
But I felt I could not keep this from you.
He told me how hard the lengthy
Train ride was on you.

He didn't want to ask you to make
The trip again.
I can imagine it was difficult.
It would be for me, at the spry young age of 69,
So I would like to make an offer.
Taking highway SH 84 north of Fort Worth
You are but 4 to 5 hours (130 miles) away by car.
I could drive up one day spend the night and drive
back the second day.

More comfortable and only 4 to 5 hours per trip
I would enjoy the drive
And selfishly would have you all to myself
for the trip.

I have taken far longer trips.
Beautiful country side

And I love adventure
I know it would be no hardship.

If this is something you believe
You could do
It would be my pleasure
To host you, and my grandchildren
Would be thrilled to see Hannah and Issac again.

Abraham folded the letter
And set it on the kitchen shelf.
The news saddened him greatly
To hear of HJ's health.

Though he had suspected as much
From the tone of the last few letters.
The car had been extremely comfortable
And only few hours he was sure would be
less tiring.

Stirring the bed springs to song
He climbed into bed,
And gave it to the Lord.
"I will do as you guide me Lord"

Chapter 18

Rarely sleepless
Abraham tossed and turned.
HJ failing!
It was too soon.

He had so many questions,
So much to learn,
So much to talk over,
Such a dear friend.

Please Lord if it be your will
Spare him a while longer.
Till I am a stronger servant for you
Till I understand more.

Slowly Abraham realized,
It was God's business
And everything would
Be in Gods time.

Abraham's job was faith,
Trust,
To believe

And give thanks.

Sleep overtook Abraham
As it turned midnight,
And he slept the deep sleep of the righteous
Assured of God's care.

Morning did come early
For the 81 year old.
He was almost late for breakfast,
And felt the tired in his bones.

Thinking about the trip
Was scary
He had to remind himself
How much easier it would be in Edgars Buick.

He talked to Hannah and Isaac,
They decided to pray for HJ,
Were excited about the trip,
And immediately started making plans.

Abraham decided to write
HJ and let him know.
He also would write Reverend Dobson
About speaking at his church.

His first letter was to Edgar
Setting a date 3 weeks in the future,
The second to Rev Dobson.
Then he was ready to write HJ.

Chapter 18

Early afternoon Abraham
Decided he'd do a little front porch sitting.
It wasn't but a few minutes
Before he drifted of to sleep.

He woke to the worried stares of Isaac and Hannah.
Abraham never slept during the day,
Abraham reassured them he was fine
Explaining his sleepless night.

He promised to go to bed early
And they seemed happy,
Though he caught some concerned looks
Throughout the rest of the day.

After supper while the children
Gathered around the radio,
Abraham formed his thoughts,
And, pencil to tongue began.

My dear brother HJ

I have been longing
To visit again.
And after a generous and kind
Invitation from Edgar,
It has become possible to
Come to Fort Worth again.

In approximately 3 weeks
Myself and the children

Will arrive by car in your
Beautiful City.
I find myself starving for a cup of coffee and
your company.

I'm in search of a closer relationship with our Lord.
I want the security the assuredness
Of knowing His will.

Sometimes I feel distant,
Removed,
I know fully it is my feelings
Not fact.

For the Lord never deserts me,
I am safe in the palm of His hand.
I will not be dropped
Or snatched from is Love.

And yet the fears persist,
The devil does not sleep,
Nor miss an opportunity
To play on my fears.

How are you my friend?
I so look forward to this visit
I hope to spend more time with you
Than previously.
I need your wisdom and company.

Your brother in Christ

Chapter 18

Abraham

Abraham read and re-read Genesis
For tomorrow mornings Bible study,
He prayed for God to use his tongue
And speak to the children.

Hannah and Isaac were soon turning off the radio,
Abraham got his bedtime hugs
They prayed together as usual
And headed for bed.

Bedspring song sung as Abraham
Pulled up the sheets,
He kept a quilt close by
For the nights we're getting a little chillier.

Sunday morning as they dressed Abraham noticed
New ribbons in Hanna's hair.
He complimented her
And she blushed.

She used her egg money wisely
And had some savings.
She had started raising some new chicks
To replace those that were headed for the
kitchen table.

He didn't monitor her spending.
Isaac's piglet sales were all put back
For a certain 22 rifle

At the Mercantile.

He knew who the ribbons were for
And smiled.
Isaac was growing at an amazing rate
And his overalls were above the tops of his shoes.

Seems they just bought a new pair a couple of weeks ago.

Sunday Morning the five children were there,
And today Becka read the 4th chapter of Genesis.
They talked about the murder and being their brothers keepers.

Abraham asked them why killing Able was wrong.
Barth said it the Bible says so.
So Abraham asked where does it say so?
Several hands in the air and the Ten Commandments was called out.

Abraham said "there weren't any Ten Commandments,
Till Moses, many years later"
There was silence
And questioning looks.

"Cain knew he was wrong,
Not from any rules,
There was nothing written,
It was from his heart"

Chapter 18

Abraham said "I have prayed about this
I have thought a lot about this
And the only way he could have known
Was from God.

God put it on his heart"
Again silence.
But this time they seemed to understand
Listening to God's guidance .

After the Bible study
Abraham went to find Mr Finnegan
Barths father.
He asked if he could spare Barth for a week
Because he had done such a good job before.

Abraham asked if he might hire Barth to watch
after the farm and animals
While they were away
Mr. Finnegan agreed without hesitation

Abraham then found Barth and the deal was struck.
Abraham was comforted
Knowing he would do a good job.

Time passed quickly,
A new dress and new overalls,
A new suitcase for Abraham,
The old one barely finished the last trip.

Abraham made arrangements

For Edgar to spend the night in Aspermont's only
boarding house.
Mrs Hodges had a fine home
And was thrilled to have such a distinguished guest.

Abraham paid the $2.50 room rental in advance
And they headed home.
They had picked Thursday to leave
Meaning Edgar would arrive
Wednesday.
They all would be eating supper
In the Cafe that night.

Abraham thought a lot about HJ that night.
His health, what he would do if he was in HJ's place,
He felt the boredom and loneliness
Might sap his will to live.

He remembered HJ's enquires
about a book of their letters.
He decided to take all of HJ's letters with him,
Maybe they could give HJ's some purpose.

Wednesday was busy packing and
Hannah filling the picnic basket.
They left home at four to meet Edgar for supper,
A shiny new Buick sat outside Mrs Hodges house.

Edgar,
As charming as ever,
Was so glad to see them.

Chapter 18

They walked from The Hodges house
To the cafe,
Good honest fare
With homemade apple pie
And a slice of cheddar cheese
Melted on top.

They cut the visit short due to the
Coming trip,
And were soon at home
Last minute packing and bed.

The familiar spring squeaks and cafe food,
And Abraham quickly dosed off.
Waking only to Othello's broken
Attempt at announcing dawn.

He met a sleepy Hannah in the kitchen
Helped get breakfast started,
And with Isaac up they thanked the Lord for food, church family
Friends and a safe trip.

The road was better to Aspermont
Now days,
So the trip was faster.
Soon they were safely parked behind Newt's office,
And walking down the street to Mrs Hodges.

Edgar and the Buick changed the trip experience completely.

Edgar said his trip yesterday was only
Just over four and a half hours,
And his new Buick gobbled up the road.

Abraham's seat was the most comfortable place he
had sat in a long time
With plenty of leg room.
He and Edgar were soon in deep in conversation.

HJ's health was an early subject.
Edgar said it wasn't a bad report,
It was just noticed in the group.
A pronounced frailty of late.
At almost 95 years of age
It just seemed time was catching up
And the members of the men's group
Were more aware.

Edgar said that the men's group
Had also insisted on paying for the gas for the trip.
Though a meager amount they all wanted to do
this out of love for HJ
And respect for Abraham.

They were quiet for a while as
The Buick swallowed up the miles.
Fields, trees and farms flashing by
And to Hannah and Isaac's joy,

Burma shave signs.
The first, attached to a fence post proclaimed,

Chapter 18

"No Lady likes",
A 100 yards or more
"To Snuggle",

Then what seemed as if forever
"Or Dine",
The children kept repeating it
So they wouldn't forget.
"Accompanied by",

On a tree in a wooded are by the road
"A Porcupine".
They giggled and laughed
Until they saw "Burma Shave".

They asked what Burma Shave meant.
Abraham explained it was a shaving cream
And Edgar explained it was what they called an advertisement.

They we quiet and watched for more,
As Abraham and Edgar
talked of faith which had been on Abraham's mind of late.
And Edgar admitted to wondering about value and purpose of his own life.

Abraham stated that he believed
Their only value was in their Father.
There worth was established by His sacrifice,
They were paid for.

Earthly value was transient
In a fallen world.
Only God's worth is important and lasting,
"At least in my view".

Edgar replied "indeed I know this well,
Yet I still need reminding".
"Funny how child-like faith is so difficult, and
yet child-like fears and insecurities are easy and
always at hand".

Three more sets of Burma Shave signs and the
Forth Worth city limit
Signs, rolled into view.
It was a shock how fast time flew
And how short the trip.

Edgar's home,
As beautiful as ever,
Was a welcoming sight.
They unloaded and went inside.

They had been welcomed at the door by Ben
Who had evidently been counting the minutes,
Till Isaac arrived, at least according to his mother.

After unpacking and cleaning up
Edgar asked if Abraham would like to visit HJ.
Abraham immediately agreed
and they were soon off to The Home.

Chapter 18

The veranda was a little less full
When they arrived.
Probably though still summer
It was a little chillier as evening came on.

But there at the table by the stairs was HJ
Still all in white, informed by phone one the visit,
Waiting with a huge smile.

A warm lingering embrace,
And with slightly overflowing eyes
HJ Said "Abraham, Abraham
My dear dear friend,

I thought I'd not see you again.
Edgar dear brother in Christ such a kind
heart you have
To facilitate this visit".

HJ led them into a small reading room
With overstuffed chairs and they sat,
With cups of coffee,
Talking of God, divine love, personal worth, and
satan's attacks.

Edgar made to leave
And both HJ and Abraham begged him to stay.
There was a coffee refill for Abraham,
And a change to hot tea for HJ and Edgar.

HJ said "I can only assume a good friend
broke trust
And informed you of my decline,
And apparent frailty".

"I'm afraid I am losing weight,
And am not sure why,
My balance grows more unsure
But I love life no less".

Abraham had been take aback
Upon seeing HJ when they arrived.
It was apparent he had aged quite a lot in just
under a years time.

Edgar said "in all fairness I must confess, out of
love for you both,
It was I that informed Abraham of my concerns
Regarding your health".

It would been beyond bearing for me
Not to give you each an opportunity to speak
once more of the Lord with each other."

They spoke more in depth
Regarding living a Christ-like existence,
The devil encouraging self doubt and
Satans use of self to undermine God's love.

It soon grew late and they said goodbye until
the morning.

Chapter 18

Abraham promised to spend the day
And HJ stood on the steps and waved goodbye in the soft Veranda lights.

A tearing of the heart even for the short time
Till morning.
Surely this is what a brother in Christ must be.

Chapter 19

Abraham had enjoyed his time with HJ.
It was so good to see him,
But there was no doubt the weight loss
had contributed to his frailness.
He could not help the feeling HJ was giving up
and he didn't know why.

Maybe feeling useless,
Maybe boredom,
Or it could be a health problem
HJ failed to mention.

Anyway, tomorrow he was going to bring
the letters
And see if he would be interested
In the book.
It would be time consuming.

No spring noise, a strange bed.
Towering ceilings must be 12 feet.
The trip and visit left Abraham tired
So it didn't take long to fall asleep.

Early noise from downstairs
Led Abraham to the kitchen for coffee.
The house was truly beautiful
Victorian he thought.
Deep rich woods and floral wall papers, beautiful,
But Abraham was a man of simple tastes.

He preferred his old farm house
Though he had to admit,
On cold winter nights,
With freezing winds,
An indoor toilet would be a true comfort.

He had reached the coffee pot before Edgar,
So he sat staring into the backyard.
Full of flowers
and an arbor of Wisteria,
It would be a lot of work to keep this up.

There were times when Abraham felt
Lost,
Disconnected,
More so in Fort Worth than at home.
He didn't feel as close to God here
As he was in the barn loft.

So it must be Abraham
That allowed the difference.
What was it?
A longing, a missing, a loneliness?

CHAPTER 19

He sat at the table by himself,
folded his hands together,
Bowed his head low
And prayed.

"Lord touch my heart
Breath on me,
Unblind my eyes,
Touch this old servant's heart.

I would find shelter in Your arms,
Peace in Your presence,
Strength in Your love,
Help this poor sinner, for without You Lord
I am naught."

He kept his head bowed and was silent.
Finally he heard the kitchen floor creak,
He said "thank you Lord for I know it's done,
Amen",

And raised his head.
Edgar said "Please forgive my intrusion
I didn't notice you were in prayer,
until I walked into the room".

Abraham replied "think nothing of it I had finished prayer.
The Lord and I were just having some quiet time",
"Are you recovered from the trip?".

Edgar said "that is not an unusual distance for me,
So I usually recover swiftly
I feel pretty good.

We can have breakfast
Giving HJ time too as well.
Then I can take you,
I know HJ will be excited".

They ate,
Drank coffee and Abraham said,
"There are times I feel apart
From our Lord.

It's not a distancing,
Not a doubting,
More a loneliness,
A disconnection.

I am in need of a reminder
Of the relevance of God
In my life,
His significance.

I would get in touch
With what I have been given.

The pain free breaths He allows,
The ability to stand and walk,
A heathy long life,
The colors and depth of my vision.

Chapter 19

Friends in abundance,
God's gentle guiding hand,
Hannah and Isaac,
Betsy's strong deep abiding love for 52 years!

I am humbled,
And embarrassed,
How can a man so greatly blessed
Feel distant"?

Edgar was quiet for a moment,
Knowing Abraham
Really wasn't asking,
But making a half statement half question.

"I believe Christians often find themselves
In this predicament" said Edgar,
"When outside worry and happenings
Pull to much at our attention".

They both were quiet,
Listening to the stirrings
Of Hannah and Isaac
As they readied for the day.

The sun occasionally peeked through
The clouds,
The garden glistened,
And they were silent.

Finishing their coffee

They left for HJ's.
Driving down the tree lined avenues,
Edgar asked no questions
about the small leather pouch Abraham carried.

Streets shiny from an early morning rain,
Steamed as the sun finally came out
from behind the clouds.
It was going to be a humid day today.

It was not a long drive,
Many beautiful houses and buildings,
Between his denomination and HJ's book royalties,
He was afforded a very nice retirement home.

Soon the three sat in the corner of the
dining room,
High ceilings and slow moving ceiling fans
Made it more than tolerable.
They sipped morning coffee and went over their
blessings.

It would be hard to say who was more blessed,
A great place to be.
Edgar excused himself,
Though retired, he often helped out
At the Seminary and would speak there today.

Soon, the cleaning crew needed their table,
so they moved to the veranda.
Swapped from coffee to ice tea.

Chapter 19

A rare treat for Abraham.

Abraham laid his worn leather pouch
On the table.
Then he said " HJ my friend do you remember
when you spoke of writing a book of our letters?"

HJ smiled "indeed I do!
I also remember you didn't respond
So I let the idea go".
Abraham nodded "well I have been praying of late".

"If our personal enlightenment,
could benefit someone else,
it would be a sin to keep God inspired
prayer and conversations private.

If you are still up to the task,
I have brought your letters,
for I believe it would take both side of the correspondence
to give a complete picture".

"I would love to!" cried HJ.
I agree it would be more complete
With both parts of the correspondence".
They sat discussing the letters
In depth, through lunch and into early afternoon.

Softly and during a quiet moment,
HJ's chin slid down to his chest

And a soft snore was heard.
Abraham took the time for himself
To feel the breeze from the fans.

He studied HJ's sleeping face.
Clean shaven, finely chiseled,
He thought, he was probably considered a good looking man
In his time.

Truly a rare friend,
With this openness between them,
A once in a lifetime meeting.
A friend sent from God.

He thanked God for these blessed times.
Low sounds of conversation,
Ice tinkling in sweating tea glasses,
And Christian fellowship.

In a while HJ opened his eyes
And sheepishly apologized.
For his nap
Abraham said "if at 95 years
Of age you can't nap, then when can you?"

Abraham then said
"I have had a thought of late
Hither-to unspoken.

You know,

Chapter 19

I have been watching our country
And their sympathies are often with
Murders and robbers.

Machine Gun Kelly,
Bonnie and Clyde, Pretty Boy Floyd
It seems to me the larger the country,
The more the lines between right and wrong
are blurred.

It concerns me for I think the
Changes are slow enough to
To sneak up on a good man,
And catch a sleeping Christian unawares".

HJ, was quiet,
Then said "a prospect, gone unrecognized by me!
I have not paid attention to this tendency
Of aggrandizing law breakers.
Truly it is insidious

A good Christian must be ever vigilant
For satan does not sleep,
his serpent-like arrival
Often goes unnoticed".

The conversation was comfortable
Two of so many God fearing men
On this veranda,
After years of
Knee-bound service to their Lord.

Edgar appeared with the twilight,
HJ waved goodbye from the steps,
As Edgar and Abraham headed home
For rest.

The children were excited at the evening meal,
Reports of who they were with and what they did
Tales of sights they'd seen
Antics and laughter.

Then Edgar said
"Isaac will you tell Abraham
what y'all will be doing
After lunch tomorrow?"

"Yes sir, a Bible study sir"
Edgar then asked "and who will be leading
this Study?"
"I will sir".
Edgar smiled and asked again " who will be there?"

"Hannah, Ben, Estelle, Mary, and Jud sir".
Edgar turned to look at Abraham
though still speaking to Isaac,
"I think that a wonderful idea young man".

Abraham was caught by surprise,
And said "Well done Isaac, I'm proud of you,
I will pray for you to be led by the Lord".
Hannah and Isaac's hugs were welcomed
Before they headed up stairs for the night.

Chapter 19

Edgar and Abraham sat quietly for a few moments,
Then Edgar said " four of my grand children
attending a mid-week Bible study, is a first.
I know they are being brought up with the
teaching of our Lord,
but such Christian examples as Hannah and Isaac
I covet for my Grand children".

Abraham said " I often find my self inspired
by their childlike faith".
Hand shakes and Abraham left Edgar
to close up the house,
and they both went up to their rooms.

Morning found HJ and Abraham
On the now familiar veranda
Speaking to a few of HJ's
Resident friends, three retired pastors
And a missionary.

With the second cup of coffee
The conversation turned to the upcoming book
And HJ began by saying "I spent
A large part of the night excited and in prayer
about our book".

I have, after much prayer, a suggestion I feel
important.
I believe we need to give a framework, a background for these letters.

I believe that information regarding the authors of the letters
can give credence and explanation to the letters.

How do you feel about this?"
Abraham sat quiet for a view minutes, then spoke,
"it is obvious you have thought a lot about this.
I too think it wise.
To try and deliver a message from God without a
picture of the deliverer might not be as effective".

"So my friend HJ, where do we begin?"
And the two men, began.
One with pen and several pads,
The other describing farm, animals, house, garden
and so much more.
So passed the next three days, morning to night.

Edgar, Reverend Dobson and several
Others attended the Sunday morning services at
Reverend Dobson church.
The 800 in attendance was the largest
group of people
Abraham had ever seen much less spoken to.

However he found himself very calm.
For he intended to remain quiet and listen to the
Lord speak.
He would be just the vessel, the voice chosen
by the Lord.

Chapter 19

He spoke on the subject he and HJ had discussed earlier,
The subtle ways we as Christians can be lulled into spiritual slumber.

After the service Abraham stood next to Reverend Dobson
At the church door and shook hands,
For what seemed like forever.
Abraham thanked everyone for their kind words

But said later to the small men's group
I know these are kind and well meaning people,
however thanking me for the message is like thanking the violin
For the song. "it was the Master violinist that deserved the praise".

Sunday afternoon and all day Monday was
Spent with Abraham talking and HJ writing.
Tuesday they would head back to home
and the farm.

Abraham was very tired.
So much talking, so many questions by HJ.
Four notebooks completely filled front to back,
He was looking forward to silence.

A difficult parting from HJ.
Accepting the fragility
And briefness of life on earth,

Many thank you's and promising to write.

So all goodbyes said they headed westward.
Hannah and Isaac watching for Burma Shave signs,
And Isaac and Edgar talking about the Lord.

After a lull in the conversation,
Abraham found himself waking
from an impromptu nap such as HJ's.

He found Hannah had slid a Afghan
she was crocheting between his head
and the window as a pillow,
Such a kind loving gesture.

He thanked her and apologized to Edgar
Who excused it saying he enjoyed the quiet time.
They arrived in Aspermont by noon.
Due to their early morning departure

Edgar said he would be going back to Fort Worth
instead of spending the night.

He could be home in time for supper
And he was to teach some Lectures
Tomorrow in the afternoon,
giving him time to rest before speaking.
They said their goodbyes,
Loaded their truck
And headed for the farm.

Chapter 19

Never was there a more welcome sight
than that old farm house.
His heart was moved
and Abraham felt over␣whelmed.

Animals happy, stalls clean,
garden weeded it looked as good or better than
when they left
That Barth was a fine young man.

Their intentions to gather around the radio
were discarded.
Supper cleaned up all three headed for bed.
It had been a blessed week of experiences
and visiting,

But this trio were tired.
The springs barely sang at all,
And no one had a hard time falling
Asleep.

Chapter 20

Othello's crow was cracked and weak
But the sun rose on time.
Deep greens with just a few spots of red and gold
beginning to show,
A welcoming sight through the back screen door.

Hannah, still sleepy eyed
Lit the kindling in the stove,
And started the morning coffee.
Abraham asked about her time in Fort Worth.

She told of their experiences
But admitted she preferred the
The farm simplicity,
And of course Barth was near-by.

Breakfast was richer more filling,
Eggs fresher,
Coffee blacker,
Home!

He owed a visit to Jeroboam,
A walk in the orchard,

Check the firewood pile,
For the coming fall.

Routine.
Comforting, reassuring,
Abraham was blessed,
No envy in him.

He had promised HJ,
To write of thoughts and occurrences,
Past and current ,
On the farm.

Abraham decided to write one page a day
To keep from feeling overwhelmed,
And do his part for the book,
There were a lot of memories.

And, as Abraham always did,
He kept his word.
One page every day,
On the ninth day he became concerned.

The stack of papers were becoming
Unwieldy
So he wrote his letter.

My dear friend HJ

Our time together was so so valuable, yet still too short,
And the cost is dear

Chapter 20

For I miss you the more.
As well as our ice teas on the veranda.

Today it is a glass of cool clear well water
In the kitchen.
The table top, blue bonnet oil clothed,
With salt and pepper shakers,
And the sugar bowl.

Backdrop for this missive
To say all is well.
I am enclosing some memories.
Please let me know if there is too much.

This week
I was sad.
This week my mind was full of Betsy,
And a longing to go home.

I asked God,
"When I ask a question Lord,
Why do you not answer YES or NO
In some Godly voice?

Maybe to easy?
A loss of mystery?
It is a child's question I know Lord,
But I also know, you don't mind that I ask".

Would it break some heavenly rule?
What would be the dire consequences

*Of our Heavenly Father,
using the words YES Abraham or NO Abraham?"*

*In a quiet voice the Lord answered me,
"God's Yes's are bigger than yours.
His yes's come with, it'll be the right thing for you,
it is My plan for you, you will be enriched,
blessed, and so much more".*

*"Your YES word is human, a child's word,
Leaving room for, great, is it good for me?
Will I like it? Can I afford it, will the conse-
quences be good?"*

*"Your NO word, also human, leaves open,
why not, did I do something wrong?
please can I, and much more"*

*"God's NO is so wonderful, it means,
It is not right for you,
It is not part of the path I have chosen for you,
the treasures I have stored up for you are so
much greater".*

*I actually think more, now when I make a request.
My next statement to God should be one of thanksgiving
and praise
Because I know no matter His answer
I will be the better for it.*

Chapter 20

I will continue to write of mine and the children's life here,
until I run out of memories or you call halt.

I hope you are not working to hard my friend

Your friend
Abraham

Enveloped, sealed and addressed,
The puffed package, awaited the next trip to
Aspermont.

He dressed for bed
And blew out the light.
The comforting bedspring song
Precursor to sleep.

There were tears in the morning,
Othello didn't call the sun.
His crow of late had been weak,
And often he had been confused about dawn.

Hannah
Said it was silly to cry over a dried up old rooster,
But breakfast was accompanied
by the sound of quite a few sniffles.

Soon even Abraham had to admit a little sadness.
Othello truly had been a magnificent
Cockerel in his day.
He lived a lot longer than most,

Must have been over twelve years old.

There were other roosters,
But none so mighty.
Abraham was a little surprised
By his own sadness.

That morning Hannah and Isaac
Insisted Abraham
Have another cup of coffee,
While they did breakfast clean-up.

Isaac fed Jeroboam and Ruthie
Before Abraham could.
Then he and Hannah buried Othello
By the side of the barn.
Isaac carved Othello's name
into the barn wood.
Abraham watched quietly
As they stood for a moment
Heads bowed.

Abraham in the back doorway
head bowed.
Thanked the Lord for his time
With these two souls
Such a blessing.

It seemed Hannah and Isaac
were both a little more solicitous
than usual,

Chapter 20

Maybe a little fearful.

Abraham thought he knew why,
 So he said at lunch
"It seems to me, there is something worrying you two,
 Do you think we should speak of it?"

Much protestation,
Uncomfortable denials and then,
Lunch was finished in relative silence.
Abraham waited.

Chores done, working on
School assignments
Abraham had chosen for them,
He heard a sniffling.

Abraham walked into the parlor where
they studied
Sat in his chair
And said, "I feel, as a family,
you need to share your troubles with me".

Isaac was the first to speak saying
"We don't want you to die!",
Then they both started to cry.
Abraham held out his arms
and they both crowded onto his boney old knees.

He wrapped his arms around them
Saying "there, there.....there, there".
When the crying subsided,
Abraham said ""everything's going to be alright".

"I guess losing the old man Othello made you sad
and you thought I might die too?"
"Well don't worry about this old man,
I plan to be around a whole lot longer"

"In Rooster years Othello was a whole lot older
than I am".
They stayed in his lap for a while longer,
But he had to shoo them into
The kitchen for some after pie and milk.

Not because he was hungry,
but he didn't want them to see how hard it was for
him to stand.
A lap full of growing youngsters
Wreaks havoc on a eighty three year olds legs.

He didn't want them to worry or feel bad
About it.
That was probably one of the best moments
of his life!
So much love!

Though Abraham did think about it.
He knew God was taking care of them
He didn't worry,

Chapter 20

But it did spring to mind on occasion.

Saturday morning there was a knock
At the screen door.
Unusual to say the least
Abraham was drinking coffee as

Hannah fixed breakfast,
Isaac was fetching up some well water.

Walking into the parlor Abraham could
See Barth, hat in hand through the screen door.
Abraham waved "a come on in"
And offered him a seat at the breakfast table.

"Would you like some breakfast we've got plenty,
and Hannah is a fine cook"
Abraham said as Hannah poured Barth's coffee,
Hannah's hand shook just a little.

Barth readily accepted and ate a hardy breakfast,
And after more coffee they moved to the
front porch.
Barth was quiet for a moment
Then spoke up.

"My father said I was to discuss this with you
as a man, so I would like to offer myself to
work for you,
Mr Graham, and Hannah, and Isaac as well

Doing any chores no matter the size, on
y'all's farm".

I do not want pay,
it would be part of my Christian ministry,
but it would also be to show you
I am a hard worker and of good character,

and though Hannah and I are young,
I would like to earn your respect and trust,
so I might court Hannah with her permission of course
when you think we have reached the right age."

And then he sighed as if winded.

Abraham was quiet for several minutes,
Barth patiently waiting for his reply.
Abraham then said,
"and you have talked this over with your father?
He can spare you?"

Barth replied "yes sir"
Abraham said I believe we need Hannah's
approval as well
don't you think?
Barth agreed immediately.

Abraham called Hannah,
who immediately appeared through the front door,
much to quickly to have been anywhere else

Chapter 20

but just inside the door listening.

Barth has made us a proposition,
that I think you need to approve of.
And he turned to Barth.
Barth repeated his offer while Hannah looked him
right in the eye.

When he finished Abraham asked her,
"would you accept Barth's courting,
once I feel you two are of the correct age?"
Hannah replied "Yes sir", right away.

"Will you both agree to never be alone together
without I or Isaac with you, at any time?"
This time they both agreed.

"Well Barth" Abraham stuck out his hand,
"I believe we have a deal".
Hannah returned to the kitchen
And Barth and Abraham sat on the porch m
to talk about what could be done.

Monday's Aspermont trip
Allowed the purchase of five gallons
Of red barn paint.
Two large brushes two gallons of paint thinner
As well has groceries.

A letter from HJ and two bulky letters posted
Abraham could think of nothing else to tell HJ.

He offered to buy lunch for Hannah and Isaac
But Hannah said she had some canning to do,
And Abraham knew
Barth would be coming over
today at noon to work.
So they made it a fast trip.

As Hannah, Barth and Isaac
Unloaded the truck.
Abraham sat down to read HJ's Letter
Upon opening
A slip of paper floated to the table top.

A check from Winslow, Hathcock and Sons
Publishing Company
Made payable to Mr A Graham!
50% of the royalty advance on a book
By Abraham Graham and HJ Foroon.

$1750!
Abraham just sat and stared at it.
He had no idea the book was done
He turned to read the letter.

Abraham my dear friend

What I would not give
For the coolness of that well water
On my lips,
You wrote of.
And the feel of those blue bonnets table-top

Chapter 20

Under my finger tips.

Often I must rein in my envy,
For it is a hungry steed,
Racing into other pastures
Leaving behind my fields over-flowing with blessings.

Our book,
Our checks,
Your message,
And God given wisdom.

I took the liberty
of sending the first four Chapters,
All that I had finished at that time, to my Publisher.

He loved it.
He sent us each a check for $1750
An advance on our royalties.
I am now finishing the eighth Chapter.

I will mail you the first five for your approval
And any changes you deem necessary,
This weeks end.

I am having a wonderful time
Writing about you three.
Such a fulfilling pleasure,
The farm,
What an amazing life.

I hope I have not taking to many liberties
Or waxed to poetic.
I am depending on your opinion
To keep me on target.

I temporarily chose the title of
"Letters Between Friends",
But the publisher felt it was a little nondescript,
Any suggestion would be appreciated.

I loved your thoughts on the Lord's "Yes and No".
We, God's Children, are so short sighted.
The future being unknown to us
We blindly ask for whatever we think we want.

Ignoring consequences,
Values,
Or even Christian ethics.
As children "We just want it".
We bare no blame for our childishness
For "Our Father" is forgiving
And understanding.
However it is ours to remember and grow from His revelations.

Thank the Lord for his wisdom and discernment,
So much of what I thought I wanted
I know now would have hurt me.
So much I have received has been far better than what I thought I wanted.

Chapter 20

I am hoping to have the book completed soon
With your suggestions and revisions,
We could get it to the editor
In the next three or four weeks.

I am anxious to see it in print.
I am convinced of the spiritual values
And lessons.
I believe they will be of great value to readers.

The veranda is almost empty
As I sit here writing.
The paper chatters in the wind,
Dusk starts to hide
The first fallings of red and gold.

It have been blessed beyond my wildest dreams
By your deep and abiding friendship.
I could ask the Lord
For no more.

A few hardy souls and I
Linger.
I, wrapped in my heavy wooden shawl,
Am here to bid farewell to summer.

To welcome the gusty fall
And nights by the fire place.
When I will long for our conversation
And you companionship.

Write as often as you can
For I hunger for your friendship.
Expect a package shorty
Your devoted friend.

HJ

Chapter 21

The money
Unearned,
No sweat,
No labor.

If you didn't sweat
You didn't work.
If you didn't work,
You didn't earn.

Ah! but then there's God!
Gifts from God,
Discernment,
That's what Abraham needed.

Abraham had asked Hannah and Isaac
To also write out some pages of their memories,
And observations for HJ.

Between the two they had written nine pages.
Very kind and loving about Abraham, the
farm, Othello,
And the other animals.

They truly loved the farm.

Abraham had sent 37 pages
Of theirs and his memories, thoughts
and descriptions in the last few weeks
Plus many letters to and from HJ.

Just life to Abraham,
Studying, learning
Praying
A student and a farmer's life.

Hopefully God lead.
If these thoughts and revelations
Were to help someone else
It would be a blessing.
And Abraham had to consider
This money as a gift from God
To His children.
He was just God's chosen guardian.

Here he found comfort
Reassurance in,
"Money for God's Children"
He packaged up his last eleven pages.

My Brother HJ

I am aw-Struck,
Speechless!
I put the money back

Chapter 21

In case the publisher decides they don't want the book.

I read the five Chapters you sent.
None of the facts have been been
Lost or mis-construed,
Though our life in your book sounds much prettier
When you describe it.

I read the chapters to Hannah
Isaac and Barth,
All loved it and wanted to hear more.
I asked them for any suggestions,

They were quiet for a while,
Then all agreed nothing should be changed.
I then said
"Actually there is a major change I think necessary",

"It is in how we all view our lives.
If we just go about the job of living,
Getting by,
We are blind to God's everyday part in our lives.

The three of us must strive to see our lives
As you, HJ have seen it, through our words.
Such a blessed place our farm is,
Look at the home God has given us".

We are excited and looking forward
To reading the next chapters you have written,
And we all will pray for God's guidance for you,

In telling others what God has told us.

My thoughts today have been guided
To think of how I treat others in my life.
And I am embarrassed to say it is causal.
An embarrassing revelation at least.

As often is the case,
What I might see as a flash of light moment,
May be for others a "oh sure, I knew that!"
Or a "took you enough time to catch on".

Everyone I deal with
must be treated as a representative
of my Lord's,
As rare and valuable.

Everyone!

To the deaf or hard of hearing,
Would not the sound of a human voice
Be a concert?
Yet I ignore so many.

To the blind my glance out my kitchen window
Would be a masterpiece painting.
The breath drawn across my lips
A miracle
For those struggling for air.

Chapter 21

As a Christian it is our responsibility
To look at the world
Differently.
Through eyes opened by our Lord!
Now don't think I'm unaware of evil,
I am not naive.
I should with the Lords guidance
Know when to embrace, and when to turn away.

To benefit from God's blessing fully,
One must be ever vigilant, aware.
I still remember the sound of that fan
Above where we sat on the veranda.

Music,
Hannah's laughter rich, bell like,
Isaac laughter fresh, free,
Uninhibited.

None of us could think of a name
For the book,
Though many were discussed.
We feel you will make the right choice.

I have something to say about the book.
It is you and I together!
This is not a book about Abraham,
It is a book about the Lord.

We the watchers together,
We the commenters together,

The book would not be
Were it not for the both of us.

Will you please take your rightful place
In the story?

Goodbye for now my dear friend,

Yours Abraham

Barth lead the Bible study on Sunday morning,
Now 9 attendees
Some prayerful insight,
Barth was wise for a nineteen year old.

The barn was almost completely red.
Barth had already nailed down
The flapping tin,
And had asked if I thought we'd ever use the corn crib again.

I told him I didn't think we would use again,
And Hannah, Isaac and Barth asked me to stay out of the barn
The for a few weeks before my birthday.
They wanted to surprise me.

Eight more chapters arrived,
Everyone was excited.
We read four chapters Friday,
Before Barth went home,

Chapter 21

And had to wait for him to complete
His secret work in the barn
before they listened to the rest
of the chapters on Saturday.

HJ was a true story teller,
All three commented on the
Insights about God
Still no mistakes.

The church continued to grow
Many strong Christian men
Shared giving the message.
Barth and Hannah taught the
Eight to Ten year old Sunday School class.

Isaac was regularly bringing home rabbits,
Now that he had is own single shot 4-10 to go
with his 22
And had actually supplied the Christmas turkey
Hannah cooked.

On Hannah's 17th birthday
Abraham gave Barth and Hannah
Permission to court.
Nothing really changed.

But they spent more of their free time
Laughing in the parlor.
And more time talking
And porch sitting.

Barth had the farm in the best shape
It had been in since Abraham was young.
Old boards replaced
Buildings painted.

Abraham's birthday arrived,
Lots of secretive whispering,
And pancakes and fresh honey for breakfast.
Then an invitation to the barn.

Abraham had been asked to stay away
For what seemed like a long time.
Sadly it wasn't hard,
Getting up to his loft was risky at best now days.

The children and Barth
Stood him in front of the closed barn doors,
Sang Happy Birthday
And Isaac opened the doors,

At first Abraham could see nothing
But the deeply familiar
Barn breezeway and stalls,
But after a few seconds he noticed

The corncrib was gone.
It had been just past the tack room.
Something new in its place
It looked like the bottom of a staircase!

Chapter 21

Walking past the tack room
Abraham found a newly built staircase,
And very sturdy handrail sanded smooth,
Climbing into his loft.

The staircase was beautifully built.
Grabbing the hand rail
He easily climbed the stairs
Nothing had changed.

Except a medium sized bell,
It was mounted on a well made stand
With a a piece of leather reins
Attached to the clapper,
And running to his chair arm.

So much thought, work
And respect
His eyes overflowed,
He sat and stared out of the loft door.

The kids left him there
And went downstairs.
He could hear them
Talking quietly as they walked towards the house.

Abraham sat for a while
Thanking the Lord
Humbled by the love,
Amazed by the children.

A birthday supper,
Barth had stayed late to see
Abraham get his Birthday cake.
The first cake Hannah had baked.

After fresh milk and cake,
Abraham looked around the kitchen table
And said I'd like to say something
To you three.

Hannah, Isaac and Barth sat staring
at Abraham
And listening,
"I have asked God over and over,

Why am I so blessed,
You Hannah,
You Isaac,
And now, you Barth

Have become great blessings
In my life.
I am in awe
That the Lord has allowed me to know you.

I just want you to know this.
To realize how much I value you
Your Love of our Lord
Our time together."

Chapter 21

They were quiet
For several minutes
Then Hannah spoke,
"I am so thankful to our father.

When he realized
he couldn't take care of us,
He was guided by the Lord,
And God sent you".

Monday,
Aspermont Post Office,
The largest of all of the three packages arrived.
Wrapped in brown paper and tied
With twine.

The last of the book,
21 Chapters total.
Everybody was excited
To get home and read it.

But Hannah said we'd
Have to wait until Barth came
Before reading it.

It took several readings,
Several days before it was through.
Seemed like they loved it and wanted to
read it again.

They liked the new title that
HJ and the publisher had picked,
But it was still dependent
On Abraham's approval.

"Letters From a Kitchen Table".
Strange name but apropos.
The children approved
Abraham was happy with both the title and spiritual content.

That night by coal oil light
Abraham licked the point
Of his pencil,
And started.

My Dear HJ

It is apparent,
God gave you the ability to write.
To turn two old men
And letters about God

Into a story even young people
Find interesting.
I love your poetic approach,
The tenderness and love in every line.

Though I lived it
I could never have told it so well.
It shows the value of finding

CHAPTER 21

God's plan for our lives

You as a teller of tales,
Me as a farmer
And caretaker for God's children.
I spent my life studying
to pass what I learned down to these two.

I am amazed at the Lord's patience,
His allowing me to find His message
At my pace,
When I was ready.

Yes I would have less skinned knees
Bruised shins
If He were to yell in my ear,
But he always waits on me.

Strange how complicated
"Faith of a child" is.
With just what I've learned
Since the children arrived,

It will take me years to understand.
I ask the Lord
That this book you and have written
Helps someone.

Maybe a questioning soul somewhere
Will pick-up a copy of "Letters From A Kitchen Table"
by authors HJ Foroon Jr and Abraham Graham

And find some understanding.

Your brother in Christ
Abraham.

CPSIA information can be obtained
at www.ICGtesting.com
Printed in the USA
BVHW021107300922
648385BV00011B/104/J